MURDER
AT FIRST
LIGHT

A gripping Lake Pines Mystery

L.L. ABBOTT

Books by L.L. Abbott

Lake Pines Mystery Series
Murder At First Light
Death At Deception Bay
Murder Of Crows
The Dead Of Winter
The Night Is Darkest
Conspiracy of Blood

Anna Ledin Thriller Series
The Blackwater Operative
The Phoenix Code
Rogue
Blown

Teen & Young Adult
Unfollowed
Order From Karoo Bridge
Carole And The Secret Queen's Scarf

Genre Fiction
The Hotel Penn
The Plus One
Our Forgotten Year

MURDER
AT FIRST
LIGHT

A
Lake
Pines
Mystery

L.L. Abbott
www.LLAbbott.com

Large Print ISBN: 978-1-989325-61-2

for
anyone
who loves
mysteries
and who trys
to figure out
who the real
killer is before
the ending,
this is for
YOU.

Murder at First Light

Welcome to Lake Pines and the (new) first book in the Lake Pines Mystery Series. *Murder at First Light* was written to replace the original first book (*Murder on the Water*) because as the series progressed, the first book no longer introduced the characters and the town of Lake Pines in keeping with how the series unfolded. *Murder at First Light* is an entirely new story, so whether you're new to Lake Pines Mysteries or not, you can enjoy this book without fear of a repeat ending, victim or murderer.
Enjoy.

"Each person is an enigma."

1

The mist crawled across the surface, clinging to the lake and refusing to release its firm grip on the water. The fog, which was intertwined with the many islands and trees that populated Lake of the Woods, parted only slightly as Velma's boat sliced a silent path toward Half Moon Bay. She learned as a child how to travel on the lake when she couldn't count on her vision for navigation and the skill was useful during late-night trips home in storms and driving through dense fog, as she was doing now. Her father taught her to use the sound of the motor as it echoed in the thick stillness, ricocheting off trees and nearby islands, changing its pitch as she drove.

Many skills were gained over the lifetime of summers Velma spent at the lake. For instance, she was the only girl in her select group of friends who could drain the bottom end of an engine, or that could prime a water pump, and her friends teased her about being an expert when it came to splitting wood with an ax as well. Unfortunately, her father also taught her how to drink when dealing with stressful moments in her life. It wasn't a direct lesson he taught Velma and her sister Chrissy, but it was in their witnessing their father as he failed to come to terms with his crumbling law practice being absorbed by a larger firm and the turbulent end of his twenty-year marriage that they picked up the habit.

It wasn't until Velma had passed out while waiting for her youngest daughter, who was completing her Friday evening lesson at Madame Rocha's dance school, that she admitted to having a problem. That was almost eight years ago, and she was still working through the recovery steps, loitering for several years at number eight and nine, which involved making amends.

Chrissy had dragged Velma to her first meeting, and they took the first of many necessary steps toward regaining their sobriety together. Along the way, they also grew closer and learned more about themselves and each other. And Velma, for the first time in her life, felt contented when she looked in the mirror.

Her only regret was that her sister wasn't still alive to see how far she'd come.

In her sister's memory, Velma made a solemn promise to make every necessary apology by the end of the summer. Velma knew it wouldn't be a simple task, and even though she wanted to make those amends without hurting anyone, she could see no way around what she had to do.

Today would be a day of change, and the early morning sailing regatta would be the venue that would ensure everyone she needed to speak with would be in the same location.

Awkward confrontations were a necessity if she was going to go through with her plan. She just had to convince herself that it would be worth it in the end.

Except for her continued connection with Mary, many of her friendships had changed over the years, as they often do for many people. Mary was like a second sister to Velma, and they had been best friends since they were children. They held a true and lasting friendship and could even build on it ensuring their bond for their entire lives no matter what challenges each of them faced.

The cottage had also become a lightning rod for many of Velma's bad habits, and she knew the ultimate step in her complete recovery was to sell their island and find another place to spend their summers. It wouldn't be easy to convince Harrison, but in the end, it wasn't his decision to make, and in time he'd see they could build more memories and create more celebrations with their two daughters. The one thing that was a certainty was that Velma wanted to be at Lake of the Woods. It was in her blood and it was her home, and it was here she wanted her family to return and scatter her ashes when she died.

Lake of the Woods had over fourteen thousand islands, and they'd be sure to find a suitable location to build another cottage. The land was rugged and the weather extreme, but the beauty was undeniable.

Weather is what either drew people close or pushed them away from the lake. Both the beginning and end of the summer saw the relentlessness of weather shifts as the lake transitioned from an evening coolness to where the morning sunrise eventually warmed the air.

Fog, cool on her skin and tight in her lungs, reminded Velma of the days her family would arrive in early May to open the cottage. Often before most of her friends would appear. Today memories visited her from her youth, reminiscent of the hours spent with her father on the lake. The cool morning trip out to Half Moon Bay would differ greatly from her trip home, which would most likely be oppressive and muggy. But for now, the chill was settling uncomfortably in her bones and she wrapped her scarf one more turn around her neck and tucked the end into her shirt, shielding her skin from the cold.

Eventually, nature would relent to the warmth of the sun, and the fog would lift and the sky would clear. But that wouldn't be for several more hours, and she needed to secure the documents before everyone arrived at the Channel Island Summer Club.

It was early, even too early for the white-throated sparrows to begin their piercing shrill that echoed over the water. Even the crows who seemed to be trained to wake cottagers from their slumber - were also silent.

Velma turned the key, silencing the motor, and tilted the engine as she let her boat drift the last stretch into the bay. It would be a scene that most people would find eerie, however, today she found a strange comfort in the stillness. Especially since she knew that by the time evening came, she'd be dealing with the fallout of her reparations.

The beach stretched across the southern length of the isolated island, shielded by the protective rocky mound of the land. Enormous fifty-foot cliffs that acted like rudders, guided blowing storms out into the open stretch of water, and the large peak in the center of the island took the brunt of the storms in the winter. This left the soft stretch of sand sheltered and a much sought-after location for summer boaters, picnickers, and swimmers. This was a place with little hospitality or a feeling of solace, but yet, it was one of her favorite places to be.

The town of Lake Pines reserved Wolf Island for public enjoyment and use. However, several cottagers sought government officials' favors hoping to rezone the island, so they'd be able to purchase it. But the initial council members had Wolf Island registered as a nature reserve zone, which made any such changes or purchases impossible. It was on this beach and around this island that Velma spent many hours in her teenage years, exploring, partying, and suntanning, and was always one of her favorite places on the lake.

Velma waited until the boat was near the edge of the sand before she jumped from the bow and pulled it up onto the beach, preventing it from drifting away. Except for wavy clumps of wild grass that grew on the isolated stretch of land, the view was unobstructed from the rocky cliffs that crawled up to the peak in the center of the island. Small caves and crevices that nature formed in the Canadian Shield were popular for hiking and exploring and even whispered tales of hidden bodies, although none were ever found.

Eagles and cormorants safely nested on the remote island, protected from cottagers and predators. It had become a popular location for wildlife photographers, both paid and amateur, and a popular national nature magazine featured spectacular images of the island on many occasions. Bonfires weren't allowed, and only 'no trace usage' was permitted. Meaning anyone visiting Wolf Island could leave nothing behind. It's also what made the island in Half Moon Bay an ideal location for Velma to hide her secret.

The small cave she hid the box inside was near the apex of the island and Velma chose the area because it was so difficult to reach and she could conceal the small opening with a pile of rocks. She had collected the documents long before she knew how she was going to use them, and she was waiting for the right time when she could reveal the information they contained. Hiding them at her cottage wouldn't work in the event Harrison stumbled upon them, and for the same reason, their home in the city was also out of the question.

It was Mary's suggestion to hide them in the same cave they would stash beer and cigarettes inside when they were teens since they were the only two who even knew the cavern existed. Not even Chrissy was aware of their hiding spot.

Each step across the beach pulled Velma back to the hours she spent on this island. The sand was compact and heavy with the dampness of the morning fog and grains clung to the sides of her white canvas shoes as she struggled against the resistance. A thin coating of dampness covered the ground and her foot slipped under her first step off the sand, and her knee came crashing down on the edge of a rock that jutted out from the uneven terrain.

The pain sent a searing heat through her body and she cursed as the ache tightened her joint. With an uncomfortable limp, Velma continued to climb the familiar path, taking each step with caution and grabbing the base of the birch trees, pulling herself up on the rocks.

She focused on her destination and what she had planned to do later in the afternoon when the pain in her knee distracted her. She didn't see the shadow darken the rock next to her and she didn't hear the grunting as her attacker ran up the same beach and rocks she just had moments earlier. By the time she realized she wasn't alone it was too late. Velma turned around just as he grabbed her arm, knocking her off balance and tumbling down the rocky cliff, landing face down in the sand. Sharp pain stabbed at her back with each motion of her leg. Fighting against the swirling feeling in her head and blurry vision, Velma tried to pull herself to her knees and crawl toward her boat.

She struggled to get away from his trembling yells, his accusations and threats mixed incoherently with apologies as he tried to get her to change her mind. She had already refused his pleas the day before when they spoke, he fumed with each word, but she'd never imagined he would pose such a sinister threat. The sand was cold and her body shook as she pulled herself toward her boat and she cried out for help even though she knew they were alone on the island.

The sun had peered over the horizon and the fog was lifting, like it did so many mornings in her life, and she knew that the mist would slowly clear and the sun would warm the early air. Soon the white-throated swallows would sing, and Harrison would pull the cover over his ears to block out the nagging prodding of the crows urging him to wake up.

She knew she wouldn't be able to outrun her attacker and when she turned to beg for mercy, the enraged look in his familiar face left her without defense. He didn't hesitate as he raised his arm above his head and lowered it, holding the same rock she smashed her knee on earlier. Nausea crept into her stomach and her head was spinning even though she remained motionless, and the final blow came down just as their eyes locked. It would be a memory Velma would hold for only seconds before she died, but she knew her killer would carry the memory with him forever. And then everything went cold.

2

Waking up early was something Kerry was accustomed to. The busy commute and long days in Montreal encouraged her to squeeze in a run before breakfast and it was a habit she wasn't able to easily shift away from. Traveling across Canada at the height of one of the country's coldest winters was probably not the best decision Kerry had made, and her father wasted no time in sharing his concern. He said that he understood the reasons she needed to leave, even if it was only for a little while, but he wished she could've waited until the summer. He encouraged the break, believing everyone needed time to recalibrate especially considering the emotionally draining career that Kerry was in but his concern as a parent overrode his opinion.

Like most Canadians, Kerry wanted to try her hand at living out west. Vancouver, she joked with her friends, was calling her name and she needed to answer. But the real reason she was leaving was much different, and it was still difficult to talk about. Instead, she began the process of constant distraction.

Before heading to Vancouver, Kerry spent three months in the western region of Quebec where she honed her skills skiing and even considered moving to the Mount-Tremblant area. She toyed with the idea of using some of her savings to open a small café but resistance from the local authorities to yet another Montrealer setting up an unwanted small coffee shop changed her mind. From there she wove her way through Ontario until she arrived in Lake Pines in late February, which wasn't the most ideal time to show up.

A harsh blizzard and a plummeting cold mass settled over Lake Pines when she arrived. Kerry took the trip and the inclement weather in stride and booked a reservation at Fox Lodge whose brochure promised hours of winter entertainment in the 'warm and rustic lodge'. Kerry purchased a dozen novels in the local bookstore and ventured out to Fox Lodge with her fingers crossed and her hopes high.

Unease at the thought of driving her Jeep over the frozen lake's ice road prompted an offer from the manager at the lodge to bring her out himself. That was almost four months ago and during that time Kerry saw many couples and travelers come and go from Fox Lodge. Besides perfecting the art of shoeshoeing, she also replaced her morning runs with rounds of cross-country skiing over the frozen lake, meandering through the nearby islands.

Simon Phillips was the manager at Fox Lodge and he had become a much-needed dose of levity in an otherwise dark, cold setting. He was in his early thirties, lean and athletic, and had a constant playful grin. They spent several hours in the lodge, some evenings huddled in front of the enormous stone fireplace during power outages caused by winter storms. She enjoyed spending time with Simon but kept him at arm's length since she knew she was leaving in a short while and wouldn't be returning to the small northwestern Ontario town. There were many positive experiences and memories she would take with her when she left, and meeting Simon would be one of them.

She experienced the spring ice melt and the emergence of the open water from the rustic surroundings of Fox Lodge and hated that her time in Lake Pines was ending. With less than one week left in her booked reservation, she needed to squeeze in as many water activities as she could before she drove west to Vancouver. And she hoped the region's shift to warmer weather would give her that opportunity.

Simon had arranged an overnight guided canoe trip that would take her and three other guests north to explore old caves that held myths and tales of dead gold miners' ghosts. An adventure shrouded in mystery was just what Kerry needed before she left Lake Pines, and she was eager to begin the trek.

While Simon was splitting wood to restock the firebox, Kerry offered to go into town and pick up the food supplies that were ordered for their trip.

Another thing she learned while in Lake Pines was how to drive a boat. Simon insisted that she learn how to use a boat once the ice broke and the water was accessible, which included everything from the practice of tying knots, docking in a small slip to even reading charts. And although she wasn't an expert boater, Kerry was learning her way around the lake with the freedom that driving a boat gave her.

Once she finished her morning coffee on the dock and the mist cleared over the lake, Kerry jumped into the small runabout and she headed into town. A sultry wind cleared the fog and mist but was making navigation through the channel difficult as it picked up force. The boat smashed down on the surface of the lake with each misjudged turn into a wave, sending a cold spray surging over the side and soaking her face. As soon as she entered Lake Pines Bay, the force of the wind dropped, blocked by the curve of the land and the buildings on the shore. Several boats were moored in the town slips, and Kerry slowed down to navigate around the ones floating in the bay until she found a place she could dock.

Even in the winter, Kerry found the town of Lake Pines a unique setting, but the emergence of spring gave the town incredible depth and color. Scattered homes and streets twisted over hills and through valleys that surrounded Lake of the Woods. Mounting hills of Canadian Shield seemed to fold over each other as they tumbled toward the water's edge, frozen in time, and created a rustic charming feel in the small town. She loved Montreal and she was looking forward to Vancouver, but she knew after her stay was over, that she would miss Lake Pines.

Once the boat was tied, Kerry grabbed her bag and headed up the long plank, making her way to Sutherland's Supply on Main Street where Simon's order was ready and waiting. Long streams of cars nestled against the curb and she passed several people that were walking toward the waterfront, some holding steaming cups of coffee in their hands and folding chairs slung over their shoulders, and everyone taking part in the Canadian pastime of discussing the weather.

The crowd swelled while Kerry was inside Sutherland's Supply, and the plastic straps began to numb her fingers as she wiggled around the slow-moving mass of people and pushed against the gust that was blowing in off the lake.

By the time Kerry reached the bottom of the hill, she sighed at the congestion of boats that were going to challenge her novice boating skills. Suddenly, a colorful distraction fluttered from the end of the dock where a man dressed in bright red pants, a white shirt, and a blue jacket was directing a group of nervous teenagers. The only thing he was missing was a paisley ascot slipped around his neck along with a pale yellow straw hat.

He held Kerry's attention and she gravitated to where he was standing, unable to resist the curiosity.

"Good morning," Kerry greeted him, and he jumped at the sound of her voice.

He turned around and laughed when he realized Kerry was speaking to him, "Oh, good morning." He tilted his head toward the bags in her hands. "You can set those up on the third table and Elise can help you organize the food."

Kerry realized the misunderstanding and corrected him, "Oh, no, sorry these are for a canoe trip I'm going on later today. I was just wondering what the crowd was for."

His eyes widened, as did his smile, and his bushy eyebrows darted up, "The annual Lake Pines Sailing Regatta, of course!"

Kerry shrugged her shoulders, "I've only been here a little while. I've been staying at Fox Lodge and I'll be heading out in a few days."

The lively man shook his head and an astonished look crossed his face as if to say, 'how could you not know?'. He held out his arm toward the dock, "Well you must come and watch the start of the race, it's the most spectacular sight to see!" He trotted ahead and guided Kerry toward the dock where several boats were floating in the bay. As he smiled, deep lines edged his friendly face, and she followed behind curious about the regatta that was about to begin.

Strings with colorful flags stretched across the boat slips and blue banners adorned buoys floating in the bay. Even the oversized fish fountain on the edge of the shore had a crowd of people perched at the base, sitting on an array of colorful folding chairs and blankets.

"This is the annual Sailing Regatta and it heralds the summer season on the lake," he grabbed the bags from Kerry's hands and placed them on a chair, and then walked her down the length of the dock. "I'm the official race starter." He thrust his hand toward Kerry, "Name's Byron Gray, I'm also the Activities

Coordinator for the Channel Island Summer Club."

Kerry returned his greeting and introduced herself, and Byron nodded as she explained the last few months, briefly and without too many personal details.

"Wow, so you left Montreal in the middle of winter?" Byron let out a jovial laugh, not mocking, but more amusing. "Can't say I've heard of many people starting a cross-country vacation in November."

Kerry just nodded and smiled, she excluded the fact she quit her job as one of Montreal's main coroners after an emotional case.

"I can't say I've ever watched a regatta," Kerry responded, changing the topic from her past to the mass of boats floating in front of them in the harbor.

"Well, you're in for a real treat, especially since the wind had picked up," Byron exclaimed, patting his hands together. "Why don't you stay for the start of the race."

Byron ran down some boating terms and rules for the sailing race, giving Kerry a quick lesson in Regatta 101. Boats with a variety of colored sails, and each crew dressed in shirts with coordinating colors, eagerly waited for the race to begin, while several boats floated in the water ready to cheer on the sailors. Shouts of encouragement were volleyed from one boater to the other and spectators were lining up on the edge of the water and dock awaiting the discharge of Byron Gray's starting gun.

He invited Kerry to stand at the end of the dock where she would have the best view of the boats at the official start of the race and excitedly found her a chair.

"Get your camera ready," Byron suggested, almost giggling as he spoke. "This will be quite a sight to see!"

Kerry opened the video recorder on her phone and steadied her arm as Byron announced the start of the race through a red and white megaphone when a shrieking scream carried out over the water stopping the start of the festivities. Byron twisted from his perch on the podium, his starter's pistol still aimed at the sky, as everyone around him turned in the direction of the sound.

Previously seated spectators lurched from their folding lawn chairs and blankets, and congregated on the end of a dock leaning forward over the water. Some pointing down, and others covering their faces with their hands.

Kerry ran behind Byron as he dashed toward the commotion, him worrying about a damaged boat but Kerry's gut instinct telling her it was something worse. Byron pushed through the crowd and stopped dead at the end of the dock and Kerry ran up beside him, and they both blankly stared at the figure floating in the water.

3

The lifeless body of a woman drifted out from underneath the dock just as Kerry reached the spot where Byron and the crowd were looking. The body was face down, her long brown hair swirling around her head, jostled by the waves caused by moving boats in the bay. Her bright-colored top, stark against the blackness of the lake, stood out as an ambiance of death settled on the crowd.

Kerry stopped Byron from reaching down and pulling the body out of the water. She could tell by the pallor of the victim's skin that she had been dead for several hours and the time spent in the water had already swollen her shape.

"Whoever she is Byron, she's dead," Kerry whispered. "You need to call the police."

Byron didn't question Kerry's familiarity with dead bodies and nodded as he pulled his phone out of his pocket with his trembling hand. Kerry asked everyone standing on the dock to move back onto the shore, and she cordoned off the pier with a row of chairs. She assigned crowd control to two young men and asked them to keep anyone from approaching the body. They were tall enough to be a deterrent and their arms large enough that they'd be obeyed. Kerry asked three boaters to form a line so that no boats or waves would disturb the body.

She wasn't sure what had happened to the dead woman under the dock, but she was familiar enough with police procedure that she wanted to make sure the innocent curiosity of intrusive bystanders did not compromise the area.

A short while later, the murmuring of the crowd ceased just before heavy footsteps echoed over the dock. A police officer, tall and strikingly good-looking, walked through the crowd and shook Byron's hand. He had deep brown eyes and an inquisitive yet pensive look on his face.

"What happened here, Byron?" the officer asked.

Byron wiped his brow, glistening with nervous sweat, "I was about to start the race when we all heard someone scream. That's when we ran over and saw the body float out from under the dock."

The officer turned to Kerry, "And you are?"

"Kerry Dearborne," Kerry extended her hand and the officer shook it. "I was with Mr. Gray when he heard the scream."

"Did anyone see her fall in?" the officer asked.

Byron shook his head, "I didn't think to ask. Kerry said she'd been dead for a while."

The officer turned to Kerry and asked, "Have you seen many dead bodies before?"

His tone was inquisitive and not mocking.

"Unfortunately, yes," Kerry explained how she was one of the lead coroners in Montreal and was just passing through Lake Pines on her way to Vancouver. "I was in town gathering some supplies for a canoe trip and Mr. Gray invited me to watch the start of the race."

"I'm going to want you to stick around long enough to give us a statement."

Kerry nodded, "Sure, no problem."

She chastised herself for stopping to watch the race and not heading straight to the boat after she left Sutherland's Supply. Simon would expect her back soon, and everyone would be ready to leave for their trip, but she knew that there was no way she could leave just yet.

"Doctor Crampton will arrive soon, maybe you can tell him what you saw," the officer suggested. "You know, coroner to coroner."

Doctor Crampton was the coroner for the town of Lake Pines and serviced the town and several small areas around Lake of the Woods. He was easy to spot as he made his way through the crowd of regatta spectators. His puff of white hair against his pale skin made him stand out against the tanned faces of the crowd around him. His gait was slow and his steps labored as he sauntered over the lawn and then down the length of the dock. He had a kind face and a warm smile and both Byron and the police officer warmed to his approach.

"Doctor Crampton, thank you for coming down," the officer said. "I thought you'd want to see where the crowd discovered the body."

He shook both Byron and the officer's hand and then turned to Kerry, extending his hand, pale and marked with age, and introduced himself, "Doctor Crampton."

Kerry introduced herself and explained what she and Byron found when they arrived at the end of the dock. Doctor Crampton leaned forward, resting his hands on his knees, his legs bowed and his body shook, as he looked down into the water and surveyed the body floating beneath them.

He stared at the body floating in the water and placed the weight of his body on the curved ladder rail, steadying his shaking arm as he leaned forward. Kerry could tell he was once a vigorous man, possibly even athletic. But time and age had settled in his life and quieted his activities.

He glared at the floating body, and without averting his eyes, he spoke only to the police officer, "She probably tumbled in with all the crowds pushing and shoving next to the edge of the shoreline."

Kerry watched the interaction between Doctor Crampton and the police officer. Kerry sensed that the doctor wasn't used to being questioned, and the police officer who would normally respect the doctor's opinion began to reveal a shadow of a doubt.

However, Kerry had the benefit of neither incumbrance and risked offering her opinion.

"I don't think so, Doctor Crampton," Kerry interjected. "I believe she's been dead for quite some time."

Doctor Crampton bristled at Kerry's supposition and turned to the police officer, ignoring her comment, "Have the body brought to my lab and I'll examine it there."

The elderly Lake Pines coroner then turned around and walked away from the body and through the crowd, not acknowledging Kerry's observation or remark.

The officer turned to Kerry with a slight blush on his face, "He's a little stubborn, he's had no one question his work or experience."

"I didn't mean to insult him," Kerry watched Doctor Crampton stomp away. "But that victim has been in the water for a few hours and she didn't fall in because she stumbled too close to the crowd."

"I'll get your statement before you go, but don't take Doctor Crampton's attitude personally, he's just been the only one in charge of dead bodies for years," the officer said trying to soothe the sting of Doctor Crampton's irritated tone.

"In charge of dead bodies?" Kerry asked. "I'm not sure if I should laugh or cry." Kerry pointed toward the victim in the water, "That's a person who deserves to be given the respect even in her death, and nobody owns her. If she died because of an accident or foul play, Doctor Crampton could be essential in narrowing down her killer."

The officer held up his hands in defense and Byron pretended not to be listening but Kerry could see him leaning toward them as they spoke.

"I'm sorry, but he's all we have and I have to work with him as best as I can," the officer said in his defense. "If the victim died because of an attack then our officers will work to find her killer. You have my word on that."

"I'm sorry," Kerry apologized. "I shouldn't have jumped down your throat, I've just seen too many murder victims go without finding justice and I think I tend to take it too personally."

"There's no need to apologize, you obviously take a lot of pride in your job," the officer smiled as he spoke.

"Took pride," Kerry corrected him.

"Pardon?"

"I took pride in my job, I quit in November and I was just passing through Lake Pines on my way to Vancouver," Kerry explained.

"Sorry, your day had to start this way," the officer said. "Dead bodies aren't a mainstay in Lake Pines."

The comment had the desired effect, and Kerry relaxed and smiled.

The officer held out his hand, "I don't think I introduced myself. I'm Constable Peter George."

Kerry shook his hand just as a crew arrived to remove the body from the water.

Police officers interviewed the men and women who gathered along the shore watching the race, as well as the sailors and race officials around the docks and bandstand to find out if anyone and seen, heard, or noticed anything suspicious.

When did everyone arrive? Where were you when the body was found? Did anyone recognize the woman?

They leveled identical questions toward each person and the officers recorded their names along with their replies. Spectators watched, perched on the edge of the shoreline, and boaters who had arrived to view the start of the race somberly looked on as a diver slipped into the water next to the body.

Byron's face grew even paler as he watched the body being guided out from under the dock and Kerry was worried he was going to be sick. She steered him away from the end of the dock and back to the shoreline where he sat down in a chair.

Kerry leaned Byron's body forward and rested her hand on his back. She watched Constable George direct the diver in the water and the crew on the dock, and she thought back to the nonchalant attitude that Doctor Crampton approached the lifeless body floating in the water, and she had a sinking suspicion that she wouldn't be leaving Lake Pines as soon as she had planned.

4

When color returned to Bryon's cheeks, and his breathing slowed, Kerry returned to the dock where Constable George was coordinating the body's removal. The diver had surfaced and told him that the victim's clothing had become entwined in the crib.

"What is the clothing hooked on?" Kerry asked the diver.

"A piece of wire that is twisted around some logs in the base of the crib."

"Can you cut a piece of the wire and leave the clothing intact?" Kerry asked, unsure what a crib was but assumed it was the base structure of the dock.

"I think so," the diver said. "The wire's old and should be easy to snip."

Constable George instructed one officer to return to his vehicle and get a pair of wire cutters from the trunk of his car and waited until he returned.

"Let's also get the large tarp which is back at the station and we can lift the victim out of the water without disturbing any evidence," he said to a second officer, and then leaned in close to Kerry. "Just in case her death was intentional."

"Good idea," Kerry said.

Any disruption of a crime scene or a victim always posed a problem when officers needed to prosecute a suspect for a murder, and Kerry could only imagine how difficult it would be to gather additional evidence from a body found in the lake.

"Except for one time when I had to examine a body found in a backyard pool, I've only dealt with crime scenes on land," Kerry watched as they lowered the tarp beneath the body and then wrapped around her sides.

"We don't know that it's a crime scene and not an accident scene," Constable George said. "But, I understand your concern. It's always a bit more difficult to secure evidence because the water, waves, and even fish can disturb the body. A lot of what we use comes down to police work and experience with past cases."

"Have any other bodies appeared at the beginning of a regatta?" Kerry asked.

"No, I'm glad to say," Constable George smiled.

Kerry glanced over at the shoreline where Doctor Crampton was waiting for the diver to pull the body next to the ramp, his eyes focused on the dead woman as he patted his hand against his leg.

"How long has Doctor Crampton been working as the Lake Pines coroner?"

Constable George shrugged his shoulders and raised his eyebrows, "Ever since I can remember. I grew up in Lake Pines and can't recall anyone but him being in that position. Not that as a kid I was hanging around the coroner's office, it's just that it's a small town, and you kind of know most of the people in it."

The diver pulled the tarp alongside the boat ramp and two officers crouched next to the water waiting for the signal to begin to lift the body out of the water. Kerry followed Constable George and watched over his shoulder as the woman's lifeless body was removed from the lake and lowered onto a gurney.

Water poured out from the open ends of the tarp and the body sagged into the plastic forming an impression against the blue tarp. Doctor Crampton walked next to the tarp and leaned over the area where the victim's head was twisted against the plastic.

He waved to Constable George as he pointed to the victim's head, "There's a gash on the front of her head, she must've fallen into the water off the dock. I'd get one of your officers to take the names of the people who were down on the shore but it doesn't look like foul play to me. Just a terrible accident. She was probably trying to get a suitable spot for a view of the race and fell in."

Constable George responded to Doctor Crampton's suggestion with a nod, however, Kerry could tell by the look on his face that he wasn't comfortable with the quick assessment of the victim's demise.

It was obvious that Constable George was used to being a leader, and Kerry wondered if sometimes that meant making decisions that clashed with other superiors he had to work with.

"Once the body is in my lab I'll figure out who she is and then you can contact her next of kin," Doctor Crampton wiped his hands on the side of his pants and thrust them into his pockets.

He then thanked Constable George and walked back to his car, passing Kerry without acknowledging her presence with even so much as a nod or a glance.

Kerry walked over to the officers who were lowering the body onto a gurney and stood beside Constable George.

"What do you think?" Constable George asked Kerry without removing his eyes from the victim.

Kerry walked next to the gurney and examined the body. One officer handed Kerry a pair of gloves and she snapped them over her hands and was instantly reminded of the familiar feeling of working alongside her boss, Jean Lamont, in Montreal.

Using a gloved finger she lifted the clump of matted hair that clung to the front of the victim's face to get a clear look at the gash Doctor Crampton was referring to.

The blood and any debris that would've been lodged in the wound had been washed away by the lake water, at least by what she could see without a microscope. But the outline of the wound was typical of an injury that she'd seen many times during her career.

"I wouldn't be able to tell you for certain unless I was examining the wound under a microscope, but I don't believe she hit her head on the dock as she was falling into the water. The angle is all wrong and there doesn't seem to be any splinters in her skin or scrapes above her forehead," Kerry lowered the hair and examined the victim's hands and clothes. "Plus, there are no injuries on her hands, which she would have if she was trying to keep from falling."

Constable George folded his arms across his chest, "What else?"

Kerry looked at him, "Judging from the damage to her skull, I think someone hit her with something large and heavy. She didn't get this injury from hitting her head in a fall."

"Doctor Crampton doesn't seem to agree with you."

"Well, maybe you can convince him to take a closer look when he's back in his lab because I can tell you this victim didn't die because she hit her head on the dock," Kerry removed the gloves and handed them to the officer next to her.

"That's going to be easier said than done," Constable George said.

"Aren't you in charge of the investigation?" Kerry asked, but instantly regretted the question since her tone was more accusatory than was necessary.

Constable George dropped his hands to his side and pushed his shoulders back, "You're right, I am." He walked off the dock and toward his car and then turned around and called out to Kerry. "Are you coming or not?"

"Where exactly do you want me to go with you?" Kerry asked.

"You need to help me find out who that woman is and who killed her?"

5

"What do you mean you want me to work on the case with you?" Kerry was in a half jog trying to keep up with Constable George's pace.

"Will that be a problem?" his voice was soft and steady, and Kerry could tell he wasn't joking.

Kerry grabbed his arm and stopped him from walking any further, "Yes, you already have a coroner, in case you've forgotten."

"And as you've pointed out, he's probably already decided what happened to the victim."

"But that's a far cry from me being involved in any investigation," Kerry said. "Plus, what are you going to do, fire him?"

"No, I can't do that, he works for the province, but you already know that. I can only direct the course of the investigation and if I think I need a consultant then I can bring one on."

"And that won't be a problem for him?" Kerry asked. The last thing she wanted to do was to tread on another coroner's territory.

"I know I just met you but I can tell that you feel the same way I do about victims of crime," Constable George said. "Everyone deserves to find some peace, and like it or not, I have an important part to play in that."

Unease slithered down her spine at the suggestion of her involvement, and she tried to ignore her own desire to search out the truth.

"How are you going to explain my involvement to Doctor Crampton?"

"I'll say you're a visiting consultant."

"A visiting consultant? Really?"

"And you can call me Peter, not Constable George," he said. "Since we'll be working together on this case."

He continued to walk toward his car, "You'll need to cancel your canoe trip for today, I'm going to need you to examine the body later this afternoon."

"With Doctor Crampton looking on? I don't think that'll be a good idea."

"That won't be a problem since he clocks out every day at four, regardless of the workload," Peter said. "Meet me at the lab at four-thirty, it's down the street from the police station." He scribbled the address on the back of a card and handed it to Kerry. "I'll see you then."

Kerry took the card and watched as Peter climbed into the police cruiser and pulled away, leaving his team of officers to deal with the crowd, the body, and the numerous witness reports that had to be documented. Kerry collected her bags from where Byron placed them on a chair and returned to her boat and then to Fox Lodge where she informed Simon and the other guests who were waiting for her to return, that she couldn't join them on the trip.

After a brief explanation of the morning's events and the body found under the dock, Simon understood, "Before you go I'll arrange another canoe trip, you can't leave Lake Pines without experiencing the old mining caves."

"Maybe," Kerry said, but the blush in her skin revealed that she looked forward to spending more time with Simon before she left for Vancouver.

Warmth filled the air in the sheltered cove, and Kerry watched with envy as everyone piled into canoes and followed Simon along the shoreline, then eventually disappearing around the corner of the island. She retreated back to her room and changed her clothes, feeling a pull to the shimmering surface of the lake. Kerry spent the day reading and swimming and waited until three in the afternoon before she headed into town to meet Peter at the lab.

Unlike earlier in the day, the bay was free of the hoards of boats and spectators that were waiting for the start of the sailing regatta.

After the removal of the body from the lake, the race eventually got underway and, although it was under a cloud of gloom, everyone saw the sailors off with cheers and applauds.

Remnants of the banners and flags were scattered along the shoreline and across the docks where the regatta festivities had taken place. As interested as she was at experiencing her first regatta Kerry hadn't returned to watch the race but still wondered how the mood must have changed after the body was discovered. The body and Peter's coercion into working alongside him, not only dampened her interest in the race but made her feel like someone had stolen the last part of her visit to Lake Pines.

She slowed her travel into town and tried to enjoy the serenity of driving the boat on the water.

Sailboats dotted the horizon and moved around several islands, and she paused to watch them on her way into town. The spectacular view of the boats leaning into the wind, with sailors perched on the edges and hanging over the surface of the water, was both soothing and exciting to watch. The coordinated effort that each team had to have, went beyond their sailing ability and relied heavily on communication.

During the winter months, Kerry experienced the typical activities associated with the cold Canadian climate. Snowshoeing, snowmobiling, and cross-country skiing were the diversions that filled her days. Simon was even able to convince her to try her hand at ice fishing, however, only once. After a frightfully frozen afternoon huddled over a hole, she had no interest in revisiting that pastime, however, the hours spent talking with Simon were quite enjoyable and ended up being the best part of her afternoon.

Once the winter thaw began and the ice melted off the lake, Kerry was thrust into another active season on Lake of the Woods. Fishing, as well as several other water sports, surfaced with the longer days. The warmer weather also allowed

Kerry to resume her running activities which she did every morning when she drove into town, which is what prompted Simon to teach her how to drive a boat on her own since he held little interest in rising early to drive her in himself.

When Kerry arrived in Lake Pines the temperature was minus thirty-five and her Jeep almost didn't start after she stopped for dinner at the converted firehouse restaurant. Her father's protests returned to her and she began to second guess her choice of departure date from Montreal, however, within a week spent a Fox Lodge she was quickly won over by the beauty of the region. She wasn't aware that winter could be such a magnificent season so full of activity and sport. The small town was full of surprises and she was enjoying each and every one.

With summer's arrival, Kerry was introduced to another character of the small town, one that included the additional population of cottagers who arrived at different dates beginning in May. The quiet bay around Fox Lodge soon saw increased boat traffic and cottagers flooded shops and stores in town when they needed to stock supplies for their cabins. Food, broken water pumps, replacement chairs – the list was endless and was the cause for steady streams of traffic along the Main Street in the small town.

Seasonal wildlife was also making a return to the area. Ducks and Canadian Geese arrived in perfect rhythmic formation as they soared above the water and town and resumed their nesting grounds in the bays and on islands from the year before.

In addition to summer cottagers and waterfowl returning to familiar locales, young campers emerged. Some parents, exhausted with the prospect of entertaining their kids over the impending summer months were looking to relieve themselves of the chore, but most wanted to give their children the chance to spend a week at one of the most beautiful lakes in Canada.

Three summer camps were situated close to town but just far enough away that the kids who came felt like they were experiencing a wilderness adventure. Buses and cars unloaded excited children who sported bright colorful packs stuffed with clothes and towels for their week-long camping experience. Guides and camp counselors, looking a little less excited, greeted the children at the end of the Main Street dock and ferried them off in oversized boats. Such an exchange was underway when Kerry pulled her boat into the docks, as parents waved to their children who were being handed lifejackets before they climbed aboard the boats, and the children did everything they could to not look afraid. Kerry was glad the dead woman's body had been removed from the lake before the kids and parents arrived for the start of their camp experience, knowing all too well, that such an introduction to Lake Pines wouldn't sit well with most parents and would create nightmares for the kids.

Kerry made her way through the crowd of kids and parents, and walked along Main Street heading in the lab's direction. She took her time, venturing into a few stores along the way and making a note of which ones she would want to visit before she left. No matter what happened earlier that morning, her time in Lake Pines was very enjoyable and she wanted to take something with her that would remind her of her time spent in the area. She just couldn't settle on an item that could encompass everything she had experienced.

She found peace during her time at Fox Lodge and she even began to forgive herself for what happened in Montreal, just as she also looked forward to arriving in Vancouver and planning a new life for herself there.

The lab was next to the hardware store and across the street from Joe Black's coffee shop, which Kerry found and frequented during her stay in Lake Pines. The coffee was rich and the Wi-Fi was strong, both essential requirements in her life.

Peter was waiting outside the lab as Kerry turned the corner and he smiled when he saw her, "I was hoping you hadn't changed your mind."

"I didn't know that was an option," a smile crossed Kerry's face.

Peter unlocked the door and held it open as she walked through, "How did Doctor Crampton take the news of me working with you on this case?"

"As you would imagine," Peter shifted sideways and closed the door. "He was a little upset but I don't think he had enough interest to put up a fight."

"Did he examine the body already?" Kerry asked.

"He did, and he sticks by his assertion that she slipped on the dock and hit her head," Peter explained and then pointed in front of them. "The room is through there."

Peter pointed to a set of shiny steel doors and pushed them open and they walked inside. The chilly air and the smell of the examination room conjured memories from her years in Montreal.

"I asked Doctor Crampton to leave the body on the examination table for you," Peter explained.

Kerry grabbed a set of gloves from the table and snapped them over her hands.

"It doesn't seem like he did too much of an examination," Kerry noticed the victim's clothes hadn't been removed and Doctor Crampton had examined only the wound on her skull. "I'm going to need a bit more time if we're going to do this right."

"Anything I can get you?" Peter asked.

"Yeah, an extra-strong coffee from Joe Black's. We're going to be here for a while."

As she stood over the body of the unknown woman, Kerry wondered if her instincts had been correct and that Doctor Crampton had missed something important.

6

Kerry stared down at the dead woman on the steel examination table in front of her. She studied the victim's skull and the marks that surrounded the fatal wound on her head and wondered how Doctor Crampton could ignore its implications. With the body properly prepared for a thorough examination, Kerry could photograph, scan, and inspect the victim's skull under a microscope, and she was certain that the wound was not accidental.

The depressed fracture on the victim's skull was the classic result of a blunt force trauma and Kerry couldn't understand how Doctor Crampton could have missed it. Once she examined the brain, it was clear the victim was struck with much greater force than she would have received from a fall off the low dock.

"Taking into consideration her weight and height, the force that she would have hit her head on any object doesn't come near the force that would have caused this kind of damage to her brain and skull," Kerry explained the victim would have died almost instantly after being hit.

"I hate to ask this, but are you sure?" Peter asked.

"Absolutely," Kerry then pulled the magnifier close to the victim's wound. "Look here, there is no scraping or small wood fragments in or around the wound."

"Couldn't the water have washed some of the evidence away?"

"Some, yes. But it wouldn't have removed embedded particles in the wound or under the skin. The abrasions that are on the edge of the wound are distinct as well," Kerry zoomed in on the image she captured and pointed to the area she was looking at. "Those are small grains of sand, and I don't remember seeing a beach anywhere along the shoreline."

They both looked up from the magnified image and then at each other. Without words, they exchanged the silent realization that they found the victim in a location other than where she died.

"There hasn't been a beach on the town's shoreline for decades," Peter explained. "The waterfront has been so built up over the years because of tourism, that there have been just the docks and the cement wall along the park's edge for ages."

"But it's not just that, it's also the shape of the wound. If I had to guess, I'd say someone hit the victim with a sharp rock," Kerry explained. "And I'd also guess there was quite a struggle which would be consistent with the other wounds I found."

"What other wounds?" Peter leaned forward, interested in what Kerry found as well as knowing it would be vital to his investigation.

"There's a recent injury to the victim's knee, and judging by the color of the bruising and extent of the swelling, the injury happened just before she died," Kerry lifted the victim's shoulder and showed Peter the bruising that was starting on the posterior surface of the victim's neck. "You can faintly see where the victim was grabbed on her neck as well. The spacing of the bruising suggests that the attacker was a man with stronger than average hands."

"So, the victim didn't die by falling off the dock?"

"She may not even have died there," Kerry said.

"Why do you say that?"

"I examined her lungs to see if she drowned and found small dust particles. The victim was dead before her body ended up in the lake," Kerry said. "I think if you test the particles I removed from her lung tissue you may find where she was killed. The gasping of air right before she died would have sucked in the particles to her lung, and they look like they'd been there for only a short while."

"Do you have any idea what they could be?"

"Some grass or weed that spreads seeds in the spring would be my guess."

"We'll have it tested," Peter wrote a reminder in his notebook to contact the lab in Thunder Bay.

"And there's also this," Kerry held out a small evidence bag containing a thin blue thread.

Peter leaned in and looked at it, "Where did you find that? It's so small."

"It was hooked in the clasp of her wedding ring. She must have scrapped her ring against her attacker's clothing and a small fiber came loose and hooked in between the diamond and the clasp holding it to the band," Kerry put it on the table with the sample of sand and the particulates from the victim's lungs. "It's a pretty distinctive blue, and it didn't come from any of the clothing she was wearing. It may be all you have to go on since there was no trace of her attacker's DNA under her nails, which was odd, considering how long they are."

"I'll have everything tested in Thunder Bay and I'll try and put a rush on it," Peter closed his notebook and slipped it into his pocket. "Do you see why I needed your help?"

Kerry had to agree, it was odd for Doctor Crampton to miss so many signs of a murder. "Well, if it helps find out who she is or who killed her, then I'm glad I agreed to help."

"Feel like a field trip to the dock where we found the body?"

"Why not, if anything, it'll rule out the dock as the location where the victim was killed," Kerry folded the sheet over the victim's body and pushed the gurney next to the cooler storage where the bodies were kept. She pulled the handle down and a rush of cool air escaped the small rectangular chamber when the airtight seal was released. Kerry pushed the gurney forward and the legs folded underneath and slid into the chamber. She pushed the door closed and twisted the handle, engaging the tight seal once again.

A calming sense of Deja Vu washed over her and she shook it off as she reminded herself that she was just helping Peter with this one case and then she'd be leaving Lake Pines for good.

"That's it, I'll just write up what I found during my examination and fill out the form to have the particulates from her lungs tested, then we can go."

Peter patiently waited as Kerry wrote out her findings from the examination, leaving one copy for Doctor Crampton on his desk and handing the other to Peter which he folded and tucked into his pocket.

"Why don't you give me the samples and I'll get them to the provincial lab and put a rush on it," Peter held out his hand.

The question didn't need to be asked since Kerry could sense that Peter wasn't sure that Doctor Crampton would submit them for testing. Having Kerry involved was enough to test his patience, questioning his results of the cause of death was another.

Peter sealed the contents into a bag and then locked the door behind them as they left the lab and headed down to the dock where they found the body earlier that day.

The thing about small towns is that it didn't take too long to get anywhere and they were soon at the side of the water less than ten minutes after leaving the lab.

Crowds of people had thinned out and although it was getting late, the warmth from the day was still present in the air. The sweet fragrance of new blossoms and sprouting leaves scented the air along the path they walked down to the dock. Yellow police tape cordoned off a large area of the shoreline and an officer patrolled the park, discouraging gawkers and teenagers from peering into the water at the end of the dock.

Peter had a team of officers search the shoreline and the park hoping they'd find a purse or a bag belonging to the victim. The diver returned to the area under the dock and spent most of the day looking for anything that could point to either identifying the victim or the attacker who may have dumped her in the lake.

"There's still no clue who she is," Peter sighed. "There was no identification in her pockets, no purse, and no bag. The officers searching the parks, garbage cans and ditches turned nothing up either."

"Well, whoever she is, she's wealthy," Kerry said, offering her insight, not sure if it would help figure out who the murder victim was, or in finding the killer.

"How do you know that?" From what Peter could tell the victim's clothes appeared to be average summer attire that a woman her age would wear.

"Even though she's dead, I can still tell she treated herself to regular facials, which isn't cheap, and she had manicured gel nails, which means, she visits a salon regularly."

"We showed her picture to some of the regular shop owners but no one recognized her, so I'm thinking she may be a cottager or a tourist."

Peter lifted the yellow police tape and Kerry and he walked underneath and along the length of the dock. Kerry looked down into the dark water and wondered what happened to the unknown victim that she had just finished examining in the lab. She crouched next to the water and looked at the dock, examining the edge.

"There was no struggle here, and the dock was completely dry this morning which means we would be able to see any scuff marks from a body being dragged and pushed over the side."

A deafening whirring sound echoed through the bay and Kerry squinted into the sun and watched as a floatplane landed on the water. A few minutes later another one landed and a ripple of waves pushed against the cribs under the dock and splashed water up onto her feet.

"How often do the planes land in the bay?"

"Every day," Peter said. "They only take off and land in the early morning or late in the day. They try and avoid the times of day when the boat traffic is heaviest."

"Do the planes come into the bay in the same direction each time?"

"Yep, every single time," Peter said. "What are you thinking?"

"I'm thinking that the body drifted in from that direction this morning and got lodged under the dock."

Peter crossed his arms in front of his chest, "There was a heavy fog this morning so it's likely that she could've drifted in without being noticed."

Kerry pointed to the end of the bay, "If you can find a beach in that direction, then you more than likely will find the location she was killed."

"And maybe we can find some evidence that will point to the killer," Peter turned around. "Come on."

"Where are we going?" Kerry ran after him.

"If we leave now we can search most of the area around the bay before it gets too dark," Peter picked up his pace as he ran toward the police boats and Kerry followed closely behind. "And there are only a few islands with a beach close by."

Kerry jumped into the boat as Peter started the engine. As he pulled the boat out of the slip and into the bay Kerry felt a rush of adrenaline and quickly tried to suppress it, but no matter how much she tried she could feel herself being sucked into working with Peter. And she liked it.

7

The bright white Glastron was the first thing Kerry saw when they rounded the sheer cliff on the end of the island. The sandy beach was the second. Half Moon Bay was located on Wolf Island which was protected as a nature reserve by the city officials several generations ago, and Peter said along with sunbathers and hikers, it was a popular place for teenagers to throw parties.

"It's still early in the season so I'm not surprised to see that there isn't anyone here right now," Peter slowed the boat as they entered the bay.

When they neared the beach, Peter cut the engine and drifted the boat in, and then when he was six feet away, he jumped off the bow of the boat while holding the rope. Kerry jumped out the opposite side, holding the second rope, and helped him pull the boat onto the sand, although, she quickly realized he didn't need her help.

"Sorry, I'm still getting used to what to do and not do with the boats," Kerry joked. "I grew up in the city, so this is all new to me."

"Ha, you could have fooled me," Peter laughed. "I took you for a small-town girl, you seemed so relaxed here."

When the boat was beached on the sand, Peter walked over to the white

Glastron and climbed in and walked through the boat looking for signs of who it belonged to. There was no registration in the glovebox and there were no bags or purses either. The only contents inside the boat were faded lifejackets with mold spreading along the seams and two frayed towels that were probably used to wipe the soiled feet of passengers.

"Why don't we check out the beach and see if the owner of the boat is around here somewhere?" Peter jumped out of the boat, easily clearing the foot of water between the bow and the edge of the sand.

They walked along the beach, Peter calling out to see if there were any hikers or sunbathers out of view. Kerry was looking to the ground to see if she could find any sign of footprints or tracks.

"The sand's pretty churned up, it's difficult to see which direction any of the steps are going."

Peter turned his attention to the ground once he was satisfied that there were no other people on the island, "It was pretty windy today, so I'm sure that didn't help. No matter how protected the bay is, the sand still gets shifted around."

Kerry walked along the beach toward the steep rock hill and noticed the multitude of sharp rocks, many that easily could have caused the injury or bruising on the victim's knee, as well as provided easy access to the murder weapon.

The beach was mostly bare, with only a few lines of grass growing through the sand in small intermittent clumps. She grabbed the top of some blades of grass and closed her fist around them and brushed her hand up the length of the stalk. When she opened her hand, fine yellow dust coated her skin.

"This could be the place where the victim was killed," Kerry said, explaining the similarity to the pollen in the grass and the grains of sand.

"Let me call in the license number on the side of the boat and see who it's registered to, or if it's been reported stolen," Peter dialed the number to the station and relayed the boat make and model along with the alpha-numeric code on the side.

"Do you have any evidence bags with you?" Kerry asked.

Peter pulled out a few bags and handed them to Kerry and she collected some grains of sand and pollen from the plants to compare to what she found on the victim's body.

"Let's keep looking to see what else we can find," Peter suggested they walked side by side at arm's length apart as they searched the ground. It was a pattern that Peter used often with other officers during searches and one he found ensured there was no area missed.

It took them half an hour to walk up and down the main stretch of the beach searching for anything out of the ordinary.

They steered their search into the grassy knoll and walked toward the rocky path that snaked up the side of the steep hill. They walked in a specific search pattern hoping to find something before the sky changed from the light blue cover to a shadowy haze. Aside from rocks, grass, and sand, there weren't many places to search on the island, and the absence of a designated trail meant any route or path that hikers would take would be created at each step. Several rock shelves jutted out offering a pseudo step where climbers could place their feet and hands, but none so distinct that it would be an obvious route.

Kerry looked up to the top which seemed to culminate at a sharp peak, "There doesn't seem to be any destination for the climbers. Do many people even climb here?"

Peter continued to climb as he scanned from side to side, "No, most people stick to the beach because the sand is so soft and the bay is protected from the northerly wind which makes it warmer than most areas on the lake."

Kerry continued to climb until they were near the top and then Peter turned around and looked down at the ground around his feet, "Nothing has been disturbed, I don't think either our victim or the attacker made it up here if, in fact, they were on this island."

A muffled buzz sounded from Peter's pocket, and he stopped climbing and pulled out his phone. Kerry listened to one side of the conversation as Peter took down the information that was being relayed to him.

"And you're sure that's who the owner of the boat is?" Peter asked. "Uh-huh, and did you call him?"

Peter was nodding as the officer on the other end of the line spoke, not giving any indication of the news he was receiving.

"And he didn't think it was odd that he didn't see his wife the entire day?" Peter asked the officer on the other end of the line, shaking his head and rolling his eyes as he spoke. Kerry knew he had found the owner of the boat and that they were talking about the victim lying in the examination room in Doctor Crampton's lab, and the husband who seemed unaware of his wife's absence.

Peter told the officer to send a forensic team over to Half Moon Bay on Wolf Island since it has now, most likely, become a crime scene and then ended the call.

"I take it your officers found out who the owner of the boat is?" Kerry asked.

"The boat is owned by a man named Harrison Whitney, and when our officer contacted him regarding the boat, he said that his wife had left the cottage before he woke up and that this is the boat she always used," Peter descended the rocky hill, following along the same path he climbed up and Kerry walked close behind.

"What did he say about his wife being gone the entire day?" Kerry asked thinking back to Peter's question he fired at the officer on the phone.

"He thought she'd be at the regatta for the entire day and he didn't expect her back until after the closing ceremony which would be after dark," Peter explained. "In fact, last night she made a point of telling him not to wait up."

"So, what's our victim's name?" Kerry always preferred to refer to victims by their name, if they knew what it was.

"Her name is Velma Whitney and the photograph that her husband texted to our officer is a match for the one we had on file from the initial examination. The officer compared it but we'll have the husband come down and identify the body. I said I'd meet him there in an hour," Peter stopped when he reached the edge of the sand and noticed the two police boats heading into the bay. "I'll have the forensic team finish searching the island and transport the boat into town so we can examine it for prints."

The blue sky, clear from clouds, spread out above the bay. Free from any threat of rain that could hamper the search efforts. The impending lack of light would be the team's only obstacle.

Peter directed the officers toward the beach and explained where he had already searched.

"I know it's not much to go on, but I think we're looking for a rock that may have been used to kill the victim," Peter told the group.

"That's like looking for a needle in a haystack, sir," one officer said.

"I know, but it's all we have right now, so try your best."

One officer was securing Velma Whitney's boat to a tow line and he was going to return to the police depot where a forensic team could examine it in a sheltered enclosure. Peter was helping him secure the rope and push it off the sand when an officer called him over to where he was standing next to the water.

"Most of the water has washed away the track of a boat that was pulled up on shore next to these rocks," the officer was pointing to a thin depression that ran under the edge of the lapping water and only a small portion was still visible on the beach. "But it may be important."

"Good eye, officer," Peter said. "Take as many pictures as you can, and have Sam take a mold of as much of the track that's left on the beach. By the time it's dark, the water will have eroded what's left in the sand."

Peter was walking back to where Kerry was standing and noticed her leaning into a pile of wild grass that edged the beach.

"Find anything?"

"Yeah," Kerry pulled the blades of grass apart so Peter could see what she was looking at. "I think I found the murder weapon."

8

The body identification went as most do. Awkwardly, emotionally and was thoroughly uncomfortable for everyone in the small cold room. Steadying himself next to the steel gurney on which his wife lay motionless underneath a thin blue sheet, Doctor Crampton and Constable George waited for Harrison to nod when he was ready for the sheet to be lifted. It wasn't something you rushed, but at the same time, everyone wanted the dreadful process to be over.

Finished and done with.

Although he was a stranger to the cold, frightening process, Harrison knew that the moment he confirmed the lifeless figure as his wife, that he wouldn't be prepared for the upheaval that would follow. Would there be tears or screams? Would he even recognize Velma? The last time he saw her was when she reached up to turn off her light before going to sleep, flicking her long brown hair over her shoulder before she kissed him goodnight.

It struck Harrison that the antiseptic surroundings were at odds with Velma's life. The clothes she normally wore were rich in texture and accented with wild colors and patterns. Her clothes could never be described as garish, however, she would have difficulty blending in with a crowd. Especially the crowd that was prone to wearing beige pants and blue shirts with only a daring splash of red during the odd formal function, which Velma's friends normally did. They were a crowd where changes never veered to the right or to the left, and where only a slight wobble was permitted.

Clothing was just one feature of Velma's that made her stand out, the other was her striking good looks that survived her years of neglect and hours of browning under the sun. Her skin was well-attended to, which assisted in returning the years that she lost in age. She bore a natural light olive tone throughout the year, gifted to her through her mother's European roots and her sharp green eyes and rosy lips was a trait that ran down the line of her father's Scottish heritage.

The cold temperatures in the morgue amplified every sound, adding to the nervous shiver that ran through Harrison's spine. The fluorescent lights hummed above them, as one bulb had continued to flicker from the moment Doctor Crampton turned it on. With nothing to grab hold of, Harrison folded his fingers into his palms and squeezed tight, hoping it would hold down any emotional outburst at seeing his wife's lifeless body. He looked to neither the elderly doctor standing to his right nor to the tall police officer on the opposite side of the gurney when he nodded.

He let out a deep sigh and a puff of warm air hung in the space between them, and Doctor Crampton slowly peeled the cover back. The fold line of the sheet fell just below Velma's collarbone revealing her face, neck, and slender shoulders.

How Harrison loved her shoulders.

His body shook as his eyes caught the top of the examiner's y-shaped incision that was now stitched closed, Harrison only aware of what lay hidden beneath the sheet because of television shows where medical examiners and coroners searched to determine the cause of death. They were actors, however, and the sight of their waxy bodies on the screen never frightened him in the same manner. He never imagined that it would be Velma that he would witness in a similar state. Harrison made a mental note to remove the latest medical drama from his viewing line-up on his movie channel, knowing he could never watch with the same enthusiasm.

Both Daniella and Helena wanted to be with him when he identified Velma's body but Harrison insisted he do it alone, and as he glanced down at his wife, he was glad he did.

Daniella inherited many of her mother's features, but Velma's toughness and resilience were hers alone. Helena bore the characteristic Whitney pale skin, frail bones, and light hair, but her shyness was the one trait that stood aside from Harrison. The Whitney family of four was fractured for much of the time that Velma and Harrison were married, but in the end, it was Velma's strength and fortitude that brought them back together. Now they were on the precipice of a dark gorge in their lives and Velma wouldn't be here to guide them across to the other side.

Her drinking problems aside, Velma was the family's glue and had even been able to see past Harrison's years of affairs and worked to keep their marriage together, insisting that they were stronger together than apart. Harrison never would have left Velma, nor did he actively search out any of his mistresses. They seemed to find him, as odd as that seemed. Harrison was neither excessively good-looking nor successful, but his allure to many younger women seemed to be his relaxed attitude and penchant to please anyone he was with. For the women in his life, it was a means to establish their attractiveness, and for Harrison, it was a way to spend time and feel desirable. It seemed to be a weakness for him the way drinking was to Velma, and no matter how young or attentive his current flame was, Harrison could never bring himself to utter the three lone words he only ever offered Velma.

His eyes surveyed the face of his beautiful wife, and he noticed the beginnings of a bruise edging out from under Velma's hairline. It bore a soft yellow – light purple haze and was split with an uneven wound that ran across her forehead. Her skin had been cleaned of any blood or dirt that Harrison imagined accompanied the laceration, and a thick band of hair was brushed unnaturally over her forehead. An attempt, no doubt, by the elderly doctor to disguise the damage that was caused to her skull. Harrison wanted to brush her hair behind her ear, just as Velma would normally wear it, but resisted the urge.

His eyes remained transfixed on his wife's face, now waxy and dull under the poor lighting and draped with death. He nodded, hoping the doctor would understand that he was ready for the thin blue sheet to be pulled back over his wife once again. A stray tear rolled down Harrison's cheek and hung on the edge of his jaw until his repeated nods shook it loose and it fell, darkening the edge of the sheet.

Doctor Crampton dragged the material over Velma's face and covered the top of her head, straightening the folds with both hands. Instantly she disappeared under the sheet.

The officer placed a hand on Harrison's shoulder and guided him away from the gurney, out of the cold sterile room, and into a small office.

The room was painted a light green, similar to most medical facilities of the same era. Rubber toe kicks edged the wall where the frayed dark gray carpet was tucked underneath. A steel desk with a fake wood veneer was angled in the room's corner with two mismatched vinyl chairs placed in front of it. Random paper and file folders and one pen were all that rested on the top. Doctor Crampton walked into the room behind Harrison and Constable George, closed the door and wiggled his body around the desk, and plopped down in his chair.

The air was warm in the small room, but Harrison still couldn't quell the shaking in his body. He rubbed his palms together and wound his fingers through his hands as he tried to force warmth and calm back into his body. Neither, he felt, would return until he was back at the cottage with a glass of gin in his hand.

His eyes stung from the tears he couldn't hold back, and each blink of his lids scraped against the surface of his corneas. Exhaustion mixed with sadness weighed heavy on him and he wanted to be as far away from Doctor Crampton, Constable George, and especially Velma who lay dead in the next room.

The doctor tried to explain his findings during the examination and the fact that both he and the police believe that Velma's death was not an accident. Unaware that an hour earlier they both disagreed with the cause of death. Their voices were muffled and Harrison felt like he was floating above himself in the room, watching the surreal event take place. They asked if there was anyone who may have been at odds with his wife – if there was anyone angry enough to hurt her.

He shook his head and told them that everyone loved Velma. Which was true.

Then came the question he prepared himself for.

Constable George wanted to know where Harrison Whitney was during the early morning hours when his wife was believed to have been attacked. He stammered that he was in bed, and no, he had no witnesses specifically since he was alone. His daughters were both at the cottage and were still in their pajamas when he stumbled down the stairs for his first coffee of the morning. They'd be able to account for Harrison's regular late morning sleep habits and his loud snoring, which for once, would come in handy since it was unlikely that his daughters hadn't heard him.

The meeting was short, and once Constable George arranged a convenient time to speak with his daughters and search Velma's things for any indication of who may have hurt her, he walked him to his boat. Harrison declined the offer to have an officer drive him home, preferring to drift slowly as he made his way back to Braemar Island. His daughters would be waiting for news about their mother, both secretly hoping that there was a mistake, and they would need comforting. Harrison would need to find the strength that only Velma had, and he would need to explain to his daughters that Velma was gone.

The one word he thought to consciously avoid was the one that reverberated in his mind. Murder.

9

Velma Whitney lived as most cottagers did at Lake of the Woods - appearing between May and September. She was a third-generation cottager having inherited the property she lived in with her husband and two daughters. Her father was a prominent corporate lawyer from Toronto and her grandfather was a major investor of the Lake Pines paper mill. Her grandfather, Wilson Pratt, was the son of Scottish immigrants and had helped establish the mill in town which employed many of the men in Lake Pines and contributed to the businesses that fed off of the once-thriving mill's success. Restaurants, supply stores, and small businesses flourished while the mill did, but once it closed, so too did many of the businesses.

Cottagers and tourists replaced some of the revenue, but it was still no match for the jobs that were lost when the mill closed.

Many perks and benefits were available to the initial business owners in Lake Pines, one of them being that they had an unwritten first right of refusal on any land that came up for sale. As an established business owner, Wilson Pratt was privy to choice plots of land when the government began to dispose of portions of crown land. Specifically, a group of islands that was put up for sale.

The Pratt cottage was one of the first cottages built in the area and it resembled more of a house than a cabin, setting off the trend that was replicated by other cottage owners on the lake.

The two-story building was clad in thick pine siding that was painted a glistening white, accented with soft blue fascia and shutters, and had a wrap-around porch that afforded views from every angle on the island. An ornate fireplace was built in the center of the cottage, constructed from perfectly symmetrical stones that were gathered at a local quarry. It mimicked one from an ancient Scottish castle complete with carvings of two lions that flanked each side of the mantle. Their eyes seemed more forlorn than fierce, and it seemed an odd choice for a cottage in the wilds of northwestern Ontario.

The paint colors, as well as the placement of the furniture inside the cottage, remained unchanged throughout the three generations of owners. Very little had changed because no one had desired the change. The cottage and the island were a respite from the pressures of work and life in a busy city. And until Velma had taken over full-time ownership of the island with her husband Harrison, it had succeeded in removing stress as opposed to adding it.

Velma's father inherited the property and then upon his death, it was handed down to her, and since then, the Whitney family of four enjoyed fifteen summers on Braemar Island.

The island's name was a nod to the lineage Wilson Pratt believed he had in connection to the famous Scottish castle. Genealogical research failed to prove his assertion, however, the name stuck, and the mythical stature of the original owner flourished. Especially among many of Velma's friends who longed to be associated with royalty or fame.

Kerry agreed to drive out to Braemar Island with Peter where they would speak with Harrison about his wife and hopefully be able to gain some clues as to why she'd been killed. Peter was with him when he identified his wife's body and decided that any questions about her whereabouts or life could wait until morning. Harrison was extremely shaken and distraught after seeing the lifeless body of his wife, and Peter knew he needed space and time before he'd be ready to answer any more questions.

They headed north from the police dock at ten and made their way to Braemar Island, avoiding clumps of fishing boats at the mouth of the channel. Promising Kerry a scenic route, Peter guided the boat through the narrow spaces between the islands, passing through shadows of cold pockets of air and capturing scents of pine and smoke along the way. She leaned into the seat and let the breeze pull her hair back, and she squinted into the warm sunshine trying to capture her bearings. Her contentment was replaced with disappointment when Peter slowed the engine and announced they had reached the Whitney cottage. Kerry wiggled her body and stretched her neck over the top of the window and took in the magnificence of Braemar Island. Her first sight was the dock and Harrison Whitney as he waited for them to arrive.

The blood-red back of an Adirondack chair dwarfed Harrison Whitney's shoulders and he seemed oddly matched for the curved structure. His body shifted from one side to the other and the bend in his knees didn't quite reach the end of the seat, leaving his feet hovering over the dock boards. Harrison looked uncomfortable and out of place at his own cottage. It was a little past ten-thirty in the morning and he looked as if he had slept very little the night before. Kerry wasn't surprised, in fact, she'd seen so many spouses, and each reaction varied. Some crumpled into a heap of sobs, while others retreated to a zombie-like state, shielding themselves from the onslaught of emotion that was sure to follow. She learned first reactions didn't always tell a tale of guilt nor did it absolve spouses of a crime. Evidence, Kerry learned, always roused the truth in a case, you just need to look harder sometimes to find it.

From a distance, Kerry could see that Harrison Whitney wore his age worse than most. His hair was prematurely gray, fading the once dark brown hair he obviously had in his youth and failing to offer the allure of refinement. His translucent skin faded his already dull eyes and his lack of muscle tone disagreed with the weight he carried in his midsection. He pushed his distorted body from the chair and ambled toward the end of the dock when Peter nudged his boat along the side.

He feigned a smile as he grabbed the boat and helped secure it to a cleat. Kerry climbed out first, followed by Peter who left his hat and jacket on the seat. Peter introduced Kerry and thanked Mr. Whitney again for taking the time to meet with them.

"Please, call me Harry," he offered them each a coffee and they accepted, and followed him up to the cottage.

The dock was long and wide and was obviously the scene of many parties. Numerous chairs and tables were positioned on the dock with colorful umbrellas behind them, secured to heavy bases to keep them from blowing away. Half-sized barrels were overflowing with purple and white flowers and displayed the appearance of having been tended with great care and attention, as did the lawn surrounding the cottage. They followed him up the wide front steps of the porch and then inside the stately cottage. The old screen door rebounded in its frame and the bounce echoed the creak in the rusted hinges. Cool air, trapped from the evening chill, replaced the warmth of the morning air outside and Kerry shivered slightly when she stepped inside.

The bright light from outside momentarily dulled their vision as they entered the darkened cottage. Small windows were the norm when the cottage was built, with conservation of warmth being a greater concern than the view.

As their eyes adjusted, Kerry could see where the family spent much of their time. Magazines and books scattered the living room tables, and blankets were erratically folded over every arm of every chair, and a large bookshelf was stacked with an assortment of frames, games, and albums, each haphazardly stacked according to their most recent use and hurried replacement.

The dining area in contrast was pristine with each chair pushed against the table at equal intervals and candles uniformly spread across the center. However, a thin layer of dust was accumulating on the surface of the table and credenza revealing the lack of use and attention the room received.

"Thank you for taking the time to speak with us," Peter said as he took a seat in the chair across from Harrison Whitney.

Kerry sat in the chair next to the window, choosing to be an observer and not a participant in Peter's questioning. She reminded herself that she was only in Lake Pines on vacation and would be leaving in a few days. In fact, she still wasn't sure how Peter was able to convince her to give up her canoe trip and help him with this case, but it was too late to change her mind now and she was committed to helping him with Velma Whitney's murder investigation.

Harrison Whitney folded his arm behind the back of his seat and then jumped up when he realized he offered Kerry and Peter coffee and quickly left the room to get the drinks. He returned moments later with three mugs, steaming with the aroma of freshly brewed coffee, and then resumed his position in the same chair.

"You said you had some questions about Velma's day yesterday?"

Peter nodded, "Yes, but let me know if it becomes too much."

Harrison Whitney held the bottom of his lip down with his teeth and he nodded his head rapidly, as if to say, *but be fast*, and Kerry noticed his hands were shaking as he pressed them against the chair.

Peter pulled out his notebook and flipped to a blank page, "When was the last time you spoke with your wife?"

"Uh, the night before she," he paused. Not wanting, or needing, to add *the day she died.*

"Did anything seem to be bothering your wife?"

"No," Harrison shook his head. "We had dinner, and then I set a fire and fell asleep reading my book. Velma was putting together some gift bags for the regatta volunteers." He pointed to the pile of navy blue bags with gold ribbon curled around each handle. "They were supposed to get them at the award ceremony. I guess I should get them over to the club at some point." Harrison's voice drifted with the thought of needing to deal with the now irrelevant thirty-two gift bags that sat on the floor, lined against the wall.

Kerry thought back to Byron's reaction when Velma's body floated out from under the dock and wondered if it wasn't his shock at seeing a body but shock at recognizing it was Velma that caused his response.

"She woke me up when she was finished and we went to bed," Harrison explained. "Before I turned out the light she said she'd be leaving early and that she wouldn't be back until after dark when the regatta festivities were over."

"You weren't going to watch the race?" Peter asked, thinking it was strange that he'd miss such a highly anticipated event for most cottagers.

"No, the regatta was Velma's thing," Harrison said with no further explanation and a small wave of his hand.

"I hate to ask this but is there anyone who can corroborate your whereabouts yesterday morning?"

Harrison shrugged his shoulders, and Kerry noticed his hands were still shaking, "I was asleep until close to noon but both of my daughters were here all day and they can vouch that I was upstairs and that only Velma's boat was gone."

"Was there anyone who had threatened your wife or that she argued with recently?"

"No, well, not that I know of," Harrison slipped his fingers together and folded his hand on his lap. "She was quite involved in the club every summer. She was their Treasurer and handled their books. It wasn't a big job but she loved doing it."

Peter folded his notebook closed and leaned his elbows on his knees, lowering his voice as he spoke. "Mr. Whitney, your wife was killed in a manner that makes me believe it was personal and not random. Are you sure you can't think of anyone who would have wanted to hurt her?"

"No, I'm sorry, I can't."

The thundering echo of footsteps preceded a much younger version of Velma Whitney as her daughter Daniella rounded the corner. Her eyes were still red with the salty sting of tears and her jaw was clenched tight as she spoke through gritted teeth. Daniella spoke only three words, but they were determined and measured. She knew who killed her mother, and she was ready to tell them.

10

Harrison guided his daughter to a chair and she recoiled her arm at his touch as she stabbed a glare in his direction. The tension that existed between Harrison and Daniella was brimming with hate and it reverberated from their bodies like lightning bolts.

Harrison tried to calm his daughter and failed miserably as she swatted his hand from her shoulder.

Peter stood and placed his coffee mug on the side table, "Why don't you show me where your wife kept some of her personal possessions, and Kerry can speak with your daughter privately."

Peter's words were posed as a question, but everyone in the room instantly sensed it was more of a directive. Harrison nodded, almost relieved at being pulled away from needing to tend to Daniella's outburst, and walked out of the room, leading Peter up to the second floor.

Daniella wiped the tears from her face, dragging the back of her hand across her cheek, but she was unsuccessful. Her tears continued to fall and soon her skin was glistening again with a fresh flood of sadness. Kerry grabbed a box of tissue, light with its repeated use throughout the evening, and held it out to Daniella. Her face softened at Kerry's kindness and she pulled two squares from the box and dabbed her puffy face.

"You probably think I'm overreacting," Daniella said through a feigned laugh.

"There is no rule book on how you should react when you lose someone close to you," Kerry's voice, soft and soothing. "Everyone grieves in their own way."

"He said that you think my mom was attacked," Daniella jabbed her chin in the direction her father just walked, and Kerry realized that Daniella thought Kerry was with the police department.

"There's evidence that proves that, yes," Kerry structured her words carefully knowing that using the terms 'murder' or 'beaten' would be too much for Daniella to handle.

"Do you have any suspects yet?"

Kerry shook her head, "It's still early yet and we believed she died on a fairly isolated island."

"Wolf Island, right?" Daniella asked.

"Yes," Kerry sat in the chair close to Daniella and left the box of tissue on the table. "Did your mom go there a lot?"

A smile crossed Daniella's face, "A ton. She used to bring Helena and me there and tell us stories of when she and her best friend Mary would go there when they were younger."

"Helena's your younger sister?" Kerry asked. "Is she here now?"

"Yeah, but you won't get much out of her, the doctor had to give her something to sleep because she was crying so much," at the mention of her sister, Daniella's face shifted from soft contentment to that of irritation before she uttered her next words. "Plus, she doesn't want to have anything to do with our dad right now."

Kerry nodded, understanding firsthand how difficult it was to lose a mother.

"You said you knew who was responsible for your mother's death," Kerry stepped back to what Daniella said when she rushed into the room. "Can you tell me about that?"

Daniella shook her head and rolled her eyes, her ponytail waving behind her, reminding Kerry of the girl's youth, "I don't know her name, but I can't think of anyone else."

Kerry tilted her head and raised her brows, "I'm going to need a little more than that to go on."

Daniella leaned forward, and rested her elbows on her knees, and whispered, "I love my dad, but he's not perfect. My mom had her own demons, but she was working hard to get over them."

Kerry looked into Daniella's face and smiled, she wanted her to know that she was there to listen and not pass judgment.

"Do you know she's been clean for eight years?" Daniella smiled, proud of her mom's accomplishments. "It wasn't easy, but she took responsibility for everything she did and she was staying clean, even with the pressure in my parent's marriage she never once tried to sneak a drink."

"That's a huge accomplishment."

"It was, which is why it was so hard to see how sad she still was. My dad's affairs always seemed to be easy to explain away because of my mom's drinking problems, but after she became sober, I thought he'd stop."

"And you think that his affair had something to do with your mother's death?"

"Or at least the person he was having an affair with."

"Do you know who that was?"

Daniella shook her head and sat back in the chair, "He denied being involved with anyone."

"You asked him?"

"Last night when he told us that our mom was dead."

"Why do you think he's having an affair?"

"He always is," Daniella replied, as nonchalantly as she would in describing the color of her pants.

"Do you think she would have hurt your mom? Did you ever hear any threats?"

Daniella shook her head, "But I overheard my mom talking to someone on the phone about selling the cottage, and I figured it was because my parents were talking about a divorce."

"Or maybe, she was just talking about selling the cottage," Kerry suggested.

The hollow echo from the stairwell interrupted their conversation and Daniella's body tensed. Peter walked into the room first, followed by Harrison whose eyes trailed along the floor. His hands were shoved deep in his pockets and his reddened cheeks were puffy and glistening with fresh tears.

Sensing that Harrison Whitney had reached the full extent of his ability to speak about his wife's death, Peter thanked him for his time and told him he'd call if he had any more questions or information. Kerry leaned close to Daniella and told her if she ever needed to talk or had any questions that she could call as well. Daniella smiled and thanked her and then pulled her legs up on the chair and hugged her knees. Kerry glimpsed at the pain in Daniella's eyes and saw a small innocent child in the body of the young woman. There were no easy words Kerry could offer to ease her pain, and unfortunately, healing would take time.

Harrison followed Peter and Kerry to the door and stood on the porch as they made their way down to the dock and into their boat.

As Peter pulled out of the bay Kerry looked back, Harrison Whitney was still standing on the porch watching them leave. And when he finally turned around and disappeared into his cottage Kerry had a sneaking suspicion that he was shielding a secret, and she was determined to find out what it was.

11

When Kerry voiced her concerns regarding Harrison Whitney's supposed oblivion to his wife's possible detractors, Peter agreed with her suspicions. Years of police work taught Peter the skill of reading body language as well as words and neither seemed to mesh with the news of his wife being bludgeoned with a rock.

For Kerry, it was more than his shaking hands or stuttered explanation of Velma's movements the night before she died. It was the familiar sweet smell on his breath that even his strong coffee couldn't mask as well as the absence of bottles in the liquor cabinet.

"I thought I smelled it too," Peter said. "I just brushed it off to Harrison trying to calm his nerves because of his wife's death."

"Maybe, but that doesn't explain the absence of bottles anywhere on that floor. The dining room and living room both had large liquor cabinets and they held nothing except a few crystal glasses and some photos," Kerry said. "His breath had a distinct scent, but I just can't seem to place it. Either way, it just seemed a bit odd."

"I agree, which is why I think we should see how involved Velma Whitney was at the Channel Island Summer Club," Peter steered the boat north and headed toward a large island with seven finger docks extending out in a fan shape from the main dock built on the shoreline.

A one-story rustic brown building surrounded by a screened porch sat back a short distance from the shoreline and was covered in an assortment of blue, yellow, and white flags. Members were arriving with bags and tennis rackets, greeting each other with waves as they pulled up to the dock. A multitude of eyes turned their way as Peter pulled his boat with the oversized police decal and flag into one of the slips.

A young boy ran toward them and grabbed the front of Peter's boat. He helped him secure it to the dock and asked them if they needed help.

"Why don't we start with you telling me the name of the person who's in charge?" Peter asked with a smile.

"That'll be Mr. Jensen, he's the club President," the young boy pointed up to the large white building. "His office is the first door on the right once you enter the building. I think he's in there now." The young boy smiled and then ran off to catch another boat pulling into the next slip.

Peter nodded to members as he made his way toward the steps to the main building, provoking a few smiles and several stares, most of which he ignored. They reached the main building, and as if everyone had been made aware of their arrival, bodies scurried from the main lobby and out onto the deck.

The President's office was to the left of the entrance and a small brass sign pointed in that direction. A man was taping a banner to the front of his window and turned around when he heard the heavy steps of Peter's boots.

He was in his sixties – tanned, fit, and athletically handsome. His six-foot-plus frame was wrapped in a muscular tone and except for a slight redness in his eyes, he had a pleasant, welcoming face. Kerry noticed he was holding up a banner that had an image of Velma Whitney printed on the front along with a message of condolence underneath it.

"May I help you, officer?"

"Are you Mr. Jensen?"

"Yes," he lowered his arms and placed the banner on the bench outside his office. "How can I help you?"

"I'm here to ask you some questions about Velma Whitney. Do you have a moment?"

His face dropped and his eyes instantly filled with tears, and Kerry could tell the redness was caused by many hours of crying. He invited them into his office and he closed the door behind them, giving them the privacy to speak freely without being overheard by members entering or leaving the building.

"We're all so devastated about Velma's death," Mr. Jensen sat down in the chair behind his desk. "It was a complete shock to everyone."

"Mr. Jensen, we're hoping you can help us with a few things," Peter began.

"Please, call me Paul," a congenial smile stretched across his tired face.

"Ok, Paul. I'm not sure if you realize that we are investigating Mrs. Whitney's death as a homicide."

The words took him by surprise and his breathing stuttered as he tried to calm his tears, "I thought Velma slipped off the dock and drowned?"

"Our examination turned up evidence that she had been killed elsewhere and her body drifted in with the current," Peter explained.

"So, she didn't die at the docks?" Paul asked.

Peter shook his head, "I understand from her husband that she was quite involved with this club."

"Yes, she was a member since she was a kid, and then she became our Treasurer several years ago," Paul explained. "She handled all the books, donations, and club fees. We were supposed to meet later today about some funding proposals."

"Who was Velma supposed to meet with?"

"Everyone in our Executive Committee, so that would be me, Byron Gray, Heath Middleton, and Sally Gale."

Peter wrote each name down, "Were there any problems among members that you are aware of?"

"No, just the opposite," Paul beamed as he brushed away the tears from his cheek. "Everyone loved Velma. She's the reason we've been able to keep this place afloat for so long. She even got the nickname of Iron Lady because she controlled the finances so tightly."

"That must have upset some people along the way?" Peter asked.

Paul nodded his head from one side to the other, and shrugged his shoulders, "Maybe a few, but those were usually just the members that Velma held accountable for the fees they avoided paying or when they tried to short change the staff. But most of those amounts were never more than a couple hundred dollars, we're just a small summer family club."

"Do you know of anyone who would have had any reason to harm Mrs. Whitney?"

"No," Paul exclaimed. "She had a lot of people's respect, especially with everything she'd been through."

"Like what?" Peter asked, this time he flipped open his notebook.

"About eight years ago she tried to clean up her life, she stopped drinking.

She went to meetings and everything, the whole ball of wax," Paul let a small smile cross his face as he thought back to Velma. "She was really trying to make amends to the people she thought she wronged, apparently it's a step that people in AA go through."

"Were you aware of any wrongs she was trying to atone for?" Peter then pointed the question to Paul directly. "Did you ever feel you were wronged by her?"

Paul shook his head, "Her apologies had more to do with times she said the wrong thing at a dinner party, but that's all."

"How close were the two of you? If you don't mind me asking."

"We worked together every summer, but we live in different cities during the year, so we never really built a deep friendship," Paul explained and then added. "But that doesn't mean I disliked her!"

"Do you know if anything was bothering her lately?"

"No, I'm sorry, I don't," Paul folded his hands together and rested them on his desk. "She seemed so happy the last few days as she was planning the regatta after-party."

Peter thanked Paul and then asked him for the phone numbers of the other individuals on the Executive Committee, which he printed out and handed to Peter before they left his office. They were halfway down the front steps when Kerry spotted Bryon Gray and she called out his name.

"Kerry," Bryon ran over to her. "I felt so badly about yesterday, I can't believe how upset you must've been."

She recognized the redness in his eyes and the scratchiness in his throat and knew that he had been mourning the death of his friend.

"Byron, I'm helping Constable George here with Mrs. Whitney's death."

Byron's face grew pale and he lifted his hand to his mouth, stifling his sobs, "I still can't believe it was her. I couldn't get to sleep last night I was so upset."

"Did you know her well?"

"Oh, yes!" Byron exclaimed and then waved his hand in the air. "We go way back, to when we were kids. I've known her forever."

Kerry motioned Byron away from a group of people who were eavesdropping on their conversation, "Byron, we have good reason to believe that Velma was murdered."

"Oh, my!" Byron leaned forward, his voice low and whispering. "What happened."

"We're not exactly sure, we're just trying to find out if there was anyone who she was at odds with recently who may have wanted to hurt her."

Byron opened his mouth to say something and then pulled his shoulders back and pressed his lips together.

Peter stepped closer, "Byron if you know anything now would be a good time to share it."

Byron's eyes fluttered back and forth between Kerry and Peter, "She was having problems in her marriage, I think Harrison was having an affair and she may have been getting ready to leave him."

"How do you know that?" Peter asked.

"Everyone knows he's been cheating on her, every summer it's someone different. That's why he never comes around the club, no one likes him very much," Byron whispered with a sting of disdain in his voice when he spoke about Harrison. "Plus, she told me she was thinking of selling her cottage."

"Why would she have told you that?"

"I'm a real estate agent and she said if she decided to sell that she'd want to do it under the radar and she asked me to keep my ear to the ground in case there was any interest."

"Her husband never mentioned anything about a sale," Peter said, and

Kerry realized she forgot to tell him what Daniella had said.

"I'm not surprised," Byron huffed. "He may not even have known about her plan. The place is in Velma's name, she even made him sign a pre-nup leaving the cottage property out of any divorce consideration if it ever came to that."

After Byron ran through the list of members that Velma had contact with as the Treasurer, Kerry and Peter left the club with the list and returned to the station where they needed to find out a little bit more about Harrison Whitney, who was looking more and more like the most likely suspect with a motive.

12

Doctor Crampton signed the official death certificate and placed one copy in his files and sent the other to provincial records in a sealed envelope. It wasn't the first time that someone's opinion challenged him to revisit an initial assessment of a victim. But it was the first time that he was forced to reconsider a case after a subordinate disagreed with him.

It wasn't just that Kerry disagreed with him, but she did it in such an intrusive fashion that he couldn't help but feel insulted by her words. She didn't have the respect or the maturity to pull him aside and to quietly speak with him, not that he would have listened to her. Kerry Dearborne had appeared out of nowhere and had disagreed with his stated cause of death in front of Peter and Byron Gray, who seemed a little too eager for everyone to be finished.

He'd known Peter since he was a small child, initially meeting him and his mother after the death of his father, whose fishing boat was hit at night. The worst part of the autopsy was discovering that Peter's father had not died instantly but had been alive long enough that if someone had called for help, he probably could have been saved.

Routine procedures and steps were followed in autopsies when a victim was found in the water, and it was those routine procedures that helped Doctor Crampton determine that Peter's father was alive for quite sometime after the boat hit him.

It was also those same routine procedures that he had overlooked when Velma Whitney's body floated from under the dock.

Doctor Crampton promised himself that he would recognize when it was time to relinquish his position and that he'd do it before he made any mistakes. Preparations for his replacement were established with his superiors in the event he was physically impaired but not for instances where his mind would reveal a loss of focus. Deep inside he knew the real problem was the distraction of the crowd that had congregated around the dock and the limited space he had around the body. There had to be at least a couple of hundred people standing by the water and several boats floating out in the harbor waiting for the start of the race.

Waves, garbage, and even the loud noises all had contributed to his distraction. But the worst of them all was the nosey persistence of Doctor Kerry Dearborne.

He wondered if she even held the proper accreditation.

Doctor Crampton kicked the lower drawer shut on his desk, thankful for the loud hammering sound of the heavy gray metal since it helped relieve some of the tension he was feeling.

It was bad enough to be reprimanded by Kerry in front of a crowd, but it was made worse when he realized she was correct. He had reviewed her autopsy notes and then looked at the body once more himself and confirmed that Velma Whitney had, in fact, been murdered.

The blunt force trauma she sustained to her head killed her, and he agreed that she didn't even die on, or near, the docks where she had been found.

Doctor Crampton was mad, not just because Kerry was right but because it put all his recent cases in a damaging light. He feared that if either Peter or, God forbid, Kerry reported his mistake, that the province would send in another coroner to review his cases. Someone could even force him to leave his position.

One way he could avoid the glare of wrongdoing was to get ahead of any potential accusations. Doctor Crampton requested the last fifty files he worked on from storage, and he would review his procedures himself. The bodies were no longer in his lab, but he'd be able to review his records, and then he could determine if he had made the right decision in those cases. And if he found any errors, then well, he'd deal with that when the time came.

The three faded storage boxes were piled next to his desk, the file clerk leaving them in his office when Doctor Crampton sent him down to the archives to retrieve them. He would start tonight, and he would take it slow.

The only thing worse than making a mistake – was the fact that a murderer could have gotten away with a crime. And that was far more worrisome than preserving his ego.

But the fact remained that Kerry Dearborne spoke out of turn and in the presence of his subordinates and that was something he wasn't going to let pass.

Before he reviewed the files and before he prepared himself to come to terms with the fact he made a mistake concerning Velma Whitney, Doctor Crampton was going to deal with Kerry Dearborne.

He picked up the phone and dialed the ten digits he wrote on a scrap piece of paper after he called the directory for the national register for licensed coroners in the country.

Montreal was over two thousand kilometers from Lake Pines but after the first two rings and the warm melodic voice that answered with a French tinged greeting, Doctor Crampton knew he was only minutes away from determining who Kerry Dearborne was and what she was doing in Lake Pines and in the middle of this most recent investigation.

13

Daniella closed the door to the upper room in the boathouse and pulled the drapes closed. The last thing that she and Helena needed was their father to walk in and find out what they were talking about.

If years of being children of two inattentive parents taught them anything, it was that secrets have a painful way of unraveling just when you don't want them to.

Most people believed Helena was overly shy and quiet, but in reality, she just didn't like anyone in her family. Except, of course, for Daniella who she relied upon since they were children.

Nights where their mother would pass out drunk and their father wasn't home, Helena would crawl into her sister's bed to wait out the night. Daniella would read stories that would take her mind off their fright at seeing their mother so disoriented.

Peter Pan was always the book they read. It was Helena's favorite, and one that would spark her imagination and dreams that they would, in fact, find a happier place to be.

Eventually, their father would return home and find their mother either face down on the top of their sheets, or asleep in front of the television with the sound turned up to its full volume.

After calming his daughter's cries, he'd return to his wife who he'd try and coax awake to drink coffee or shower. Velma would shout slurred insults, and as most parents incorrectly assumed, they believed their hurtful words were hidden from their daughter's ears because they were in another room.

Threats of divorce followed by promises of mistresses being outed and finances being cut off replaced the images Daniella and Helena had conjured up of Wendy being carried off by Peter Pan to Neverland, where a happier life existed.

It was Daniella that Helena phoned when she rushed out of her dance class at Madame Rocha's and found their mother tilted forward, head resting on the steering wheel, and drool spilling from the right side of her mouth. She wasn't worried that her mother was sick or hurt, or even dead. They had both seen her in that state several times and knew that along with the juice box and chocolate treat their mother always brought for Helena after dance class, there was also a small bottle of clear liquid tucked in the side pocket of her purse.

Instead of calling their father, Daniella called 911. She wasn't even old enough to stay home alone, but she knew that with that call both ambulance and police would arrive at Madame Rocha's where not only would they find their mother drunk behind the wheel, but that all of her friends would see it too.

That day, and their mother's near escape from being charged, all thanks to their grandfather's high-priced law firm, forced Velma's hand to abstinence.

Since then, neither Daniella nor Helena ever had to encounter a scene such as that and they had both watched as their mother clawed her way to sobriety and worked to repair the damage she had caused.

It would take years before either Daniella or Helena fully trusted their mother, and it was only after they saw the change in her that they let down their guard.

Much more still need to be done before either of them could rest easy, but now it was too late.

Together, they had been through so much, and Helena, who only became comfortable with trusting their parents again, had walked in on their father while he was in bed with another woman, sending Helena back into a reclusive shell.

Again, Daniella was the one she called when she was in distress, and it was Daniella who was going to make the problem go away and make everything alright. Their father didn't deserve the trust and love their mother gave him, and despite her addiction, her family always came first. And he definitely didn't deserve their trust and affection.

This summer would be the summer that they'd make him pay for all the hurt and deception that he caused their mother. They would be the cause for Harrison Whitney's collapse, and they didn't care how he felt when they revealed what he had done.

Their grandfather's connections extended to their mother, and then by nature, extended to them. They had both already made the call that would see the final funds he had been promised after their mother's death be diverted from his account and placed into a sealed trust. It would be kept offshore and out of his reach.

The suspicion the police had against their father for the murder of their mother was all the two girls needed to finally agree to move forward.

Harrison Whitney was going to suffer in life the way that their mother did in her death, and they were going to make sure it happened soon.

14

After calling the members of the Executive Committee for the Channel Island Summer Club, Peter arranged to speak with them one at a time. Gaining information that could guide him in the direction of Velma Whitney's killer was the ultimate goal, and like most murder investigations, they were often solved with the most innocuous clue leading him in the right direction.

Paul Jensen offered to book the staff lounge room where Peter and Kerry could speak with them without fear of being interrupted, watched, or having their conversations eavesdropped on. He was also the first person Kerry and Peter saw when they walked in the front doors of the club.

"Morning," Paul greeted them with a smile and an offer of fresh hot coffee. "I have a room set up for you and I told the staff working in the cafeteria that you're not to be disturbed."

"Thanks, I'm sure we'll be done before noon," Peter kept his words brief and the details of his questions to a minimum. "Why don't we begin with you since you're already here."

Paul walked ahead of Kerry and Peter, leading them into the room and when they were all inside, he closed the door. The room was small with two oversized windows that faced the main sailing dock of the club. Light flooded the room and reflected off the thick rustic plank walls that were painted a bright white, contrasting the rustic exterior.

Nautical-themed lamps, candles, and fabric adorned the room. White, blue, and yellow were the repeated colors, with strikes of red as accents in several of the pieces. Kerry sat in an oversized blue and white striped chair and Peter took the matching one next to her, moving the yellow pillow to the sofa so he could sit all the way back into the seat.

Paul dropped onto the sofa and his long legs stretched under the coffee table that rested between them. He leaned into the arm of the sofa and waited for Peter to begin. The first questions were rudimentary, intended to find out how long Paul knew Velma and if they were close friends outside of their club responsibilities.

Each answer was as simple and clear as the question and elicited no other responses than pleasant ones. Paul could never recall meeting Velma because he could only ever remember knowing her. Both of their families had been vacationing at their cottages in Lake Pines from the time they were babies and since they were close to the same age, they usually ended up at the same parties or get-togethers over the years. They had never been close, nor had they ever argued.

As a teenager, Velma was quieter than Paul was and rarely took part in sports at the club like tennis or sailing. He never saw her as rude but more of a loner that just preferred to spend her time with a few quiet friends.

It wasn't until her daughters started to play tennis at the club that Velma became involved as the Treasurer, using her skill with numbers and organization to get the books systematized.

Velma had been the one to encourage Paul to take the role of the club President when the club needed a replacement. The previous member held the position for over ten years and was ready to move on and just enjoy the dock at his cottage and sailing with friends. The job of President often extended into the winter months and required hours of Paul's personal time. Filing documents, hiring staff, raising money, and looking for alternative ways to entertain members kept him busy throughout the year.

"Most of the reason for the club doing so well was because Velma kept such a tight rein on the finances," Paul explained.

"You mentioned that she was quite good at her job, and maybe even upset some members."

Paul readjusted his arm and folded it behind the back of the sofa and crossed his leg, "Upset comes in varying degrees. Some members wouldn't pay their full fees on time or would argue some food charges on their account, but those amounts never reached over a couple of hundred dollars, and wouldn't have pushed anyone to murder."

"Were there any current members in bad standing?"

"I checked before our meeting, thinking back to your comment when we first spoke, and the answer is no. All of our members' accounts are up to date and no one is in arrears."

"Was there anyone who she didn't get along with that you think may have wanted to hurt her?"

"I know it sounds contrived, but everyone here really liked her, she was always doing things for the staff or to recognize our volunteers," Paul smiled. "She even insisted on putting together gift bags for the volunteers for the regatta."

"We saw them at her cottage when we were speaking with Harrison, she was working on them the night before she died," Kerry thought back to the navy gift bags with the glossy curled ribbons on the handles.

Paul's eyes filled with tears and they spilled over his lower lids when he blinked. His fingers brushed clumsily across his cheeks, "I'm sorry, I still can't believe it."

After a few more questions, Peter excused Paul and asked him to send Byron in, who he could see through the small window in the door was pacing in the hall.

Byron sat where Paul had and stared at the space between Kerry and Peter. Spots of white appeared around his knuckles and his hands shook as he pushed his tight fists into his lap.

"There's no need to be nervous, Byron," Peter began. "I wanted to ask if you remembered anyone arguing with Velma in the last little while. We figured speaking with the people she worked closely with would be a good place to start."

Byron shook his head, "She didn't have problems with anyone here. She was a quiet member too, she only ever came by once and a while to watch her daughters play tennis or when she was doing the books."

"You mentioned that you knew that Velma was considering selling her cottage and that her husband was having an affair," Byron sat up as Peter shifted the focus of the conversation to Harrison. "That's something I'd consider very personal information. You must have been close."

Byron nodded his head, "We were friends since we were kids, we've known each other forever."

"Did the two of you ever date?" It was Kerry who asked the question, surprising Byron and catching him slightly off guard.

"No, we were just friends," Byron murmured.

Peter asked a few remaining questions, and then excused Byron and invited Heath Middleton into the room. Heath was a tall man, lacking the muscle tone and tan that many of the men who sailed at the club had attained. It was obvious from the way he carried himself that he was someone who was used to being listened to and he expected any suggestions he made to be accepted, whether he was right or wrong. A scraggly red beard with streaks of gray mostly obscured his pale face, the only indication of what color his previous head of hair was lay in the strands under his chin. The slight hue in his eyes indicated they were once a bright blue but now faded to a dull gray, with matching pockets of shade underneath. Sallow and transparent, his skin lacked the features of anyone Kerry saw enjoying the outdoors. Even people who burned and avoided direct contact with the sun had more color than he did. There was something dead about Heath Middleton, or was he just dull? She couldn't decide but one thing was for certain, he didn't look like he was eager to cooperate with any of their questions.

Body language was tough to hide but easy to read after years of dealing with people, and sharing news of death revealed many emotions. Guilt was the one that both Peter and Kerry were trained to identify.

Heath's answers were quick, short, and his tone wasn't friendly or cordial. He had only met Velma when he joined the Executive Committee five years ago upon his father's insistence that he should accept a position on the committee. His father was a large contributor to several endowment projects and wanted to make sure that his donations were protected and handled appropriately.

"He wanted to make sure that the money was spent how he intended it to be spent," Heath waved his hand in the air. "Not on frivolous things."

"Were you aware of anyone who may have quarreled with Velma? Especially over the last couple of days."

"No, but as I've already told you I am only involved with the club as a committee member, providing legal advice when needed," Heath grumbled just before he stood. "If that's all, I have my family waiting for me at the dock."

Peter stood and shook Heath's hand, "That's all my questions for now. But if you remember anything, please call me." Heath nodded his head and without saying another word, turned and left the room.

"That leaves Sally Gale," Kerry said as she read the list of executives on their list.

"That's me!" a cheery voice rang out from the short brunette that walked into the room. Her voice was cheerful and welcoming but her eyes were red with the trace of tears she had just wiped before she entered the room. Mascara rubbed the left side of Sally's cheekbone where she had tried to wipe the tears from her face, and black liner drooped down below her lids.

She wore her hair in a short style, cut just below her ears, and her curls bounced as she walked. She shook both of their hands and pulled a crumpled tissue from her pocket and ran it under her eyes just before she sat down.

Unlike the previous interviewees, Sally sat close to Peter and Kerry and leaned in as they spoke. She was both a welcome face during this arduous process and an eager talker.

When asked if she was aware of anyone who may have argued with Velma before her death, she was more forthcoming than the previous three men they had just spoken with. And Kerry guessed, more honest.

"Why, every week there was someone mad at her," Sally said. "I didn't envy her job as the treasurer. People were either pressuring her to release money for programs or sign off on some invoice when they had already committed to buying something from a supplier. She spent most of her time saying no and double-checking what was in the storage shed."

"Why would she be checking the storage shed?"

"She would make sure the invoices matched up to the items that were purchased," Sally explained. "That's why she was pushing for a more streamlined process where only one person would be in charge of collecting and storing purchases made by the club. But for the last little while, Velma was doing that, and frankly, I think she was just getting tired."

The mention of Velma's name send another flood of tears and Sally dabbed the corner of her eyes with her soggy tissue.

When Peter was sure he had received all the information he needed, he thanked Sally and handed her a card, "If you think of anything, just call."

Sally smiled as she took the card and left the room, and Kerry could hear the beginnings of low sobs as she walked down the hall. None of the three interviews brought them closer to revealing the name of a person who could have been angry enough with Velma to hurt her. Outside of minor squabbles over unpaid fees, Velma didn't seem to have any enemies at the club. But one thing was made clear after speaking with the three remaining members of the Executive Committee.

No one could ever remember seeing Harrison at the club or supporting Velma, and his affairs were never a secret well kept. And affairs of the heart can be more potent and deadly than disagreements over money. Kerry had seen it before, and she thought, maybe, it could've caused Velma Whitney's death.

15

A quick internet search of Harrison Whitney turned up both the name of his company as well as the list of court cases against him for default of payments on his business loans. The cases were eventually settled in a sealed court agreement dated a month before Velma Whitney died. What wasn't sealed were the names of the companies and people who were suing him in court.

Peter called the one person on the list whose name he recognized, hoping to gain some insight into the life, and potential problems surrounding Harrison Whitney.

The simple mention of Harrison Whitney's name was all it took to encourage Samson to talk.

Samson Jones was the owner of Starbright Plumbing in Lake Pines and had been hired by Harrison to complete work on a townhouse development project he was managing in Winnipeg and Toronto. He was remodeling a small older row of townhomes on a charming side street in Yorkville, almost so small it was forgotten. When he saw how well received it was, he decided to dive into purchasing a strip of homes in his hometown of Winnipeg and then demolished them in preparation to replicate the same design he used in Toronto.

However, he moved forward before he sold all of the homes in Toronto or received the appropriate zoning in Winnipeg which left him holding a sizeable amount of debt and no foreseeable way to repay it to the companies chasing him.

Harrison had initially met Samson when he replumbed their cottage on Braemar Island, replacing the unreliable water system with a modern solar-heated unit, and said he wanted to have someone he trusted working on his two largest projects.

He promised to pay for Samson's out-of-town lodging along with all additional costs for the project, none of which he did, and forced Samson to take him to court if he wanted to receive any compensation.

"I had to recoup my costs at least," Samson said in defense of filing the suit against Harrison. "To tell you the truth, when I saw the long list of debtors who also took him to court, I didn't think I'd ever see a dime!"

"What changed?"

"His wife called me up a couple of months ago," Samson explained. "She was furious. She found out about his debts but she couldn't get any information from the court documents or any of the other debtors, so that's when she called me, hoping I would tell her what was going on."

"What was going on?"

"Harrison liked to play the big shot and he got involved in a project to redevelop some old townhouses with a few shady developers and he overextended himself.

He kept putting off payments and I eventually cornered him and told him I wanted to be paid," Samson let out a small laugh. "He told me to get in line!"

"That's when you filed your claim?"

"Yeah, but it was several months after that when Velma called me up. I told her everything and confirmed the rumors she had already heard from one of her friends."

"She must have been mad," Peter said.

"Yeah she was, but not at me," Samson added. "She's a good person and I've been doing work for her family for years. It was her husband she was furious with."

"So, what happened after you told her what her husband had done?"

"She wrote me a cheque and then she said she was going to pay everyone else off too, so I had my lawyer contact the other plaintiff's lawyers and got the names she needed," Samson let out a deep sigh. "I feel really sorry for her, you know, being married to a louse like that."

Peter then broke the news to Samson that Velma was murdered and that they were looking for any credible reason someone may have targeted her. The upset was clear over the phone and it devastated Samson to hear of Velma Whitney's death, but he assured Peter that once she paid off all of Harrison's debts that there was no reason for any of the creditors to target her. In fact, he said, since it was a small community of tradespeople, they'd all mentioned that she was a gem for what she did. The only stipulation she ever made was that her husband was never to learn that she paid off his debts.

With new light being shone on Harrison's legal dilemma, Peter brushed aside his business associates as plausible suspects in Velma's murder.

Peter hung up the phone and explained his entire conversation to Kerry who agreed that Harrison Whitney was looking less and less innocent the more people they spoke with.

The tension that must have existed in their marriage was enough to cast suspicion on her husband, but both Peter and Kerry agreed that they needed more than just speculation before they accused him of her murder.

Money, or specifically debt, has long been a reason for murder and Kerry wondered if that was what eventually found its way to Velma on that isolated beach on Wolf Island.

"Maybe her husband found out that she paid off his debts and he was upset," Kerry said.

"How upset would you be if someone cleared your debts?" Peter asked. "Plus, he didn't know that she had done that?"

Kerry drummed her fingers on the corner of Peter's desk, which was something she did when she was trying to work something out in her mind.

"What are you thinking?" Peter sat back in his chair and folded his arms across his chest.

"Part of the AA mantra is to make amends to people you may have wronged in your past, especially while you were drinking. What if there's someone in Velma's past she wronged and when she tried to make up for what she did, it just infuriated them instead of appeasing them and they lashed out?"

"That's a good theory, but how do we find out who Velma was trying to apologize to?" Peter opened the thin file he had assembled for Velma Whitney. "Outside of her husband, who seems to have an alibi from his daughter, there is no one jumping out at us as a suspect."

"How long will the lab take to return the results?" Kerry was thinking more about the blue fiber since she believed they found the location Velma was murdered along with the rock that was used to kill her and instinctively knew it would point to her attacker.

"It'll be another day or two before we get the results from the lab and just as long until my forensic crew is finished searching Velma's boat for any evidence."

"What about that impression of the boat mark in the sand?"

"That, I did get back," Peter pushed his chair back and walked over to the coffee machine, and poured two cups as he spoke. "Judging by the angle of the seam of the hull and the depth of the pressure in the sand we think it was a fairly small boat, plus there was a clear indentation in the sand from where a trailer hook was attached to the boat and there was a distinctive dent just below where it probably smashed against a rock or a trailer."

"But you'll need to find the boat first to compare the mark?"

Peter placed the cup of coffee on the desk in front of Kerry, "Exactly."

Kerry took a long gulp of the coffee and her stomach rumbled reminding her she hadn't eaten since breakfast, "I have another idea."

Peter took a sip of his coffee and waited for Kerry to explain.

"I had a friend who joined AA, and I remember her going to regular meetings, so I was thinking, Velma may have had a group she met with while she was at the lake. There's a chance that she may have opened up to someone at the meetings."

"I hate to state the obvious, but it's supposed to be anonymous," Peter said.

"It's worth a shot. Unless you have another idea?" Kerry asked. "You must be able to find out when the next meeting is in town."

Peter opened his community police browser on his computer and entered in the search for local support meetings and he received three results.

"There's a meeting tonight at the Portage Community Center," Peter looked at his watch. "And if we leave now, we'll just make it."

16

The community center was set back from the highway and next to a small creek that ran through the east section of Lake Pines. A group of teenagers played basketball on a fenced-in court while a crew of friends cheered them on with friendly taunts and screams. The night air still held some warmth from the afternoon sun and the new grass and Balsam Poplar tree buds scented the evening air, while the conflicting mix of cigarette smoke and cherry blossoms fought for dominance in the crowded yard behind the community center in the late afternoon air.

The location of the AA meeting was posted just inside the door on the information board. Random postings filled the board, some advertising the sale of used cars, two for teens looking for babysitting gigs, and one for the sale of a litter of pups. The board held the life and social events of the small town. Notices of potluck suppers, retirement dinners, and new stores opening in town were affixed to the corkboard by a colorful blend of pushpins hoping to grab some attention from people passing through the doors. Kerry's eyes lingered over the notices, not because they were of special interest to her, but because they even existed. The process of board notices in a community center was something she missed experiencing growing up in a big city and she thought the idea somehow was comforting. Similar announcements in Montreal were made through social media and in glossy color magazines filled with big store ads that dominated the pages. The retirement of a local high school would not have registered as news the way it did here in Lake Pines.

However, the notice that held immediate interest to her was the yellow one indicating the room and time the AA meeting was taking place.

Room 12b was on the second floor and made the community center sound larger than it was. In fact, the local fire department's emergency procedures required that each room, even broom closets, have an actual room number assigned to them.

The small rectangular room was an odd choice for the AA meeting, and Kerry wondered if they held all their meetings in the same room, or if the group was at the mercy of whichever room was available and clean. The primary use for the room was for a preschool group, made clear by the oversized alphabet letters taped to the wall and the 'I do not hit' sign that was prominently displayed above images of happy children playing on a rug.

Kerry and Peter sat at the back of the room soon after they walked through the door, choosing a spot that set them apart from the group. She was glad Peter insisted on changing out of his uniform before they left his office, as they blended into the background more easily. Downturned faces of the two men sitting in the front row mirrored the mood of the people that walked in after Kerry, and sideways glances from a woman seated at the end of the row, assessed Kerry's threat to the group. These four walls offered nonjudgemental support, and no one was ready to give that up or risk it for two strangers. As the room filled, the mood shifted and people started talking. The shoulders of the once tense woman relaxed and she even offered Kerry a small welcoming smile.

Like most meetings, this one lasted an hour and a few members shared their stress at the approaching summer backyard barbeque season. Images of wine coolers and frosty mugs of ale were everywhere they looked. Grocery store advertisements selling burgers, restaurants announcing their patio openings, and even one for a commercial selling flip flops had a frosty glass of lime Margarita.

Pressure and triggers were everywhere for this group and Kerry thought of her friend Jan who must have been feeling all these same things when she stopped drinking. Kerry wished she'd gone to a meeting at the outset of Jan's struggle years ago, to understand her friend's challenges better.

When the meeting was over, most of the members spent a few moments speaking to each other at the back of the room while the moderator of the group pushed some loose paper into her bag. After listening to the members of the group speak, Kerry decided that honesty would be the best policy in speaking with anyone in this group about Velma. She also felt that it would be better to do it on her own and she asked Peter to wait downstairs.

Kerry introduced herself to the moderator and after confirming that Velma attended her group, she briefly explained what happened. The moderator, a woman by the name of Josie, fell back into her chair and reached for the small box of tissue that was perched on the corner of the desk.

"Velma's dead?" Josie wiped her eyes and balled up the tissue and tossed it into the wastebasket.

"I'm sorry to have told you this way, but you understand why I thought to come to this group," Kerry explained. "It seemed like a logical place for Velma to talk about things that may be bothering her."

Josie nodded, "But I'm not sure I can help you. Velma has been a part of our group for almost eight years, I took over as moderator about five years ago. She just came to meetings in the summer and only shared a little bit, and very infrequently. She talked mostly about how difficult the parties and socializing were becoming when she was at her cottage but never in too much detail."

"Did she ever mention anyone by name that she may have been having problems with?"

"No," Josie blew her nose. "It's the silent killer we try and warn our members about. At first, friends are supportive and understanding. They try to not drink around you and even go out of their way to have several non-alcoholic beverages available for you, but then the effort becomes too much and friends drop off or become complacent in their own habits and it's just hard to be around them."

"Was there anyone Velma spoke with or got close to? Eight years is a long time to continue to come to meetings and not connect with someone."

Josie's eyes narrowed, "Actually, there was this one man who she spent a lot of time speaking with when she first arrived this year, his name's Guy."

Kerry looked to the group talking in next to the refreshment table, "Is he here tonight?"

"No, and he wasn't here the last time Velma came and she seemed quite upset, almost like she was waiting for him."

"Do you have a last name for him?"

"We only use first names, unless someone wants to share, but the entire point is to make the process as unintimidating and supportive as possible," Josie explained.

"If I leave you my number, can you give it to him if he comes back?" Kerry handed the piece of paper to Josie. "Tell him it's about Velma."

Josie folded the piece of paper and promised to pass it along to Guy if he returned to a meeting. Kerry left the room and found Peter in the middle of a game of twenty-one with a group of teenagers, and he seemed to be winning.

Kerry leaned against the fence and watched how Peter interacted with the youth group, who had obviously grown comfortable with having a police constable around. Peter spotted Kerry outside the fence and told the group he had to leave and after a round of high-fives, he walked off the court and wiped his brow.

"Man, I thought you'd never get here," Peter laughed but something told Kerry that he enjoyed interacting with the group of teens.

"I'm starving, is there somewhere close we can grab a burger?" Kerry felt the rumble again in her stomach.

He was just about to make a suggestion when his phone rang, "Hello."

Kerry watched Peter's face twist as an officer on the other end of the line spoke. He grimaced as he ended the call and tucked the phone into his pocket.

"That was one of my officers," Peter explained. "Someone attacked Harrison

Whitney when he was in town getting some groceries and he thinks it's related to what happened to his wife."

Peter was already climbing into his car and Kerry had just opened her door, "Where is he now?"

"At the emergency room," Peter said. "Getting stitched up?"

17

Hospitals, Kerry decided, smelled the same no matter where you lived. The antiseptic coolness of the emergency room could have been in Montreal, or Halifax, or Edmonton. The tinny sounds of the intercom buried behind the rush of gurneys being pushed down the hall and smashed through swinging doors, the wheels squeaking as they tried to turn corners – all the sounds were the same.

The staff immediately recognized Peter, even out of his uniform, and a nurse directed them to the examination room where Harrison Whitney was being treated. Inside, was a bloodied Harrison Whitney holding an icepack against his forehead while a tanned young blond was rubbing his back. The closeness indicated she was neither a nurse nor his daughter.

Shock was the first expression that raced across Harrison's face, embarrassment was the second, as he pushed the woman's hand away from his back.

"Uh, I already filed a report with another officer," Harrison stammered out his words, Kerry was uncertain if he was drunk or embarrassed and unsure of what to say.

"I know, I came down because that same officer said you thought that maybe the attack had something to do with your wife's murder," Peter said while watching both Harrison and the young woman's expression.

As he expected, the woman snapped her arms in a fold and pressed them close to her chest when Peter said the word 'murder'.

Harrison turned to the woman and tried to usher her out of the room, "Can you get me some water? Thanks. I'll be done soon."

The girl shot Harrison a stern look before yanking her purse off the chair and stomping out of the room.

"Is that Helena? I never met her," Kerry asked and it impressed her that Peter hadn't even cracked a smile.

Harrison blushed a deep red, bringing the only color to his pale skin tone, "No, she's a friend."

He stammered through a few sentences making his way toward changing the topic and then explained what happened when he was leaving the grocery store. The crunching gravel was his only warning of the impending attack as he was pushed to the ground and repeatedly kicked.

"I only survived because the manager heard my screams and came running out of the store and chased off the attacker," he lowered the ice pack, uncovering the deep purple bruise that was forming around a series of minor cuts and scrapes.

"Did you get a look at your attacker?" Peter asked as he locked eyes with Harrison trying to read his reaction to his questions.

"No, but the manager did. He said he was wearing a dark hoodie and a pair of jeans, and he took off down Second Avenue when he chased him."

"To be totally honest, Mr. Whitney, it sounds like you were a victim of a mugging," Peter folded his hands behind his back. "I assure you we'll take it seriously, but I don't think it's related to your wife's murder."

Harrison dropped his chin, almost looking upset that the attack wasn't thought to be more serious and that he was simply the victim of a mundane petty burglary.

"Have you found anything else out about who attacked Velma?" Harrison's eyes stayed fixed on Peter as he asked about his wife.

"No, we're following up a few leads, but we're also still waiting for some test samples to be returned from the lab," Peter explained.

"Tests? On what?" Harrison's eyes narrowed.

Peter paused before speaking, unsure of how much information he wanted to reveal to Harrison, who he still hadn't ruled out as a suspect, "We found some pollen in your wife's lungs and some sand in her wound."

Harrison's face relaxed.

"Also, we found a small fiber from what may have been her attacker's clothing, but we're not sure."

"Fiber? What fiber? I don't remember the doctor at the morgue saying anything about a fiber," Harrison's eyes darted back and forth from Kerry to Peter.

Peter left out the fact that it was Kerry, and not Doctor Crampton who found the fiber, "It was so small, and we'd rather make sure we check everything out before we say too much. You understand."

Harrison gave a feeble nod.

"There has been something that has come up, however, that we wanted to speak with you about," Peter said.

"Sure, what is it?"

"Were you aware that your wife cleared several of your debts recently?"

Harrison's face shot up and his eyes widened, "Were you looking into me?"

"We need to explore every angle if we're going to find out who killed your wife, and a trail of excessive debts looks like a good place to start," Peter explained. "You didn't answer my question, though, did you know that your wife paid off your debts?"

"I didn't even know she knew about them," Harrison dragged his thin dirt-stained fingers across his face. "Do you think one of the guys I owed money to did this to her?"

"We're looking into everyone involved, but it would've been more likely that they would have come after you, to be honest."

The truthful realization stung, and Harrison sat up straight. "You don't think I did it do you?"

"Your wife was a wealthy woman," Kerry said. "If she died, you would have inherited a lot of cash."

"Actually, no," Harrison tossed the soggy bag of ice on the bed and it immediately darkened the pale green hospital bed sheet. "I would have been able to keep the house in the city plus a small annuity that wouldn't have amounted to very much, just a small salary. Everything was left to our girls. We both wanted it that way, and believe it or not, I had always been successful up until the last few years and had never needed Velma's money. That's not why I married her."

A shadow of emotion flashed across his face and Kerry believed that, at one point at least, he loved Velma very much and was truly shaken by her murder. However, she made that mistake once before and as a result, a killer walked free. She was going to keep guarded where Harrison Whitney was concerned.

"When we left your cottage, you said you were going to think of anyone who may have had a problem with your wife. Did you come up with anything new?"

"No, Velma didn't lead a glamourous life. She spent a lot of time with the girls and volunteering. In the summer she spent most of her time at the club helping with the books, and over the winter she worked at the women's shelter. She wouldn't hurt anyone."

By the time they were finished taking down the rest of his statement, Harrison was fatigued and ready to leave the hospital. He was halfway out the door when Peter asked him to continue to think about anyone who may have had a reason to hurt Velma and to let him know if anything came to mind.

He nodded a faint agreement and stepped into the hall, where his young blond friend looped her arm in his and they walked away.

18

Kerry awoke to the serene sound of the water gently lapping against the rocky shore that was less than twenty feet from her window. Morning songbirds of mixed varieties bounced from one tree branch to another as they warmed their wings under the rising sun. Kerry was the only guest at Fox Lodge and Mrs. Kemp, the chef-slash-housekeeper, was the only other person on the island. Simon had messaged Mrs. Kemp that the canoe trip had been extended due to the warm weather and the eagerness of the crew to venture further north, which left Mrs. Kemp and Kerry the only two remaining inhabitants at the lodge. At least for one more week, which is when planned to leave for Vancouver.

The cool morning air, blended with the warmth under the duvet covers, made it difficult for Kerry to want to get out of bed. She had never slept as well or as deeply as she had since she arrived in Lake Pines, and she wondered if it was the surroundings or her time away from corpses. Her work helping Peter with Velma Whitney's murder should be able to answer that question soon enough.

She flung the covers off her legs and slipped out of bed. After a quick shower, she dressed and joined Mrs. Kemp in the kitchen for the breakfast she prepared for them. It was the same menu every morning, however, Kerry never complained. In part, because it was so delicious but mostly because Mrs. Kemp took so much pride in doing it.

"Good morning, dear," Mrs. Kemp's voice mirrored the songbirds outside Kerry's window more than that of a seventy-five-year-old retired teacher.

Mrs. Kemp insisted that Kerry call her by her first name, however, she could never get past her father's voice and her years surrounded by older relatives that hammered in the tenents of respect throughout her youth and she refused to call her Margery.

Age was truly just a number for Mrs. Kemp. Every morning she easily traversed the wobbly dock when she jumped into the small tin boat and drove into town to shop for fresh ingredients for the kitchen, never waning or slowing down. Her career in teaching gave her the patience required to deal with troublesome guests and lodgers, and her years raising a family of five children made her an efficient and exemplary cook.

Standing five-foot-six, Mrs. Kemp was lithe and strong, not seeming to have gained the weight normally associated with retirement. Instead, she dove head-first into a second career when she retired and her husband died, leaving the energetic woman with time and vigor to spare. Her light brown hair was streaked with small strands of gray that highlighted and not dulled her appearance. Bright green eyes and a natural pink to her cheek revealed her approachable and kind demeanor and made her an easy morning companion.

"Good morning, Mrs. Kemp," Kerry pulled out a chair and sat down at the table already set with coffee, eggs, and a fresh fruit salad. "As usual, this smells amazing."

"I wasn't sure if you would want to sleep in or not, considering how quiet it is around here with everyone on the canoe trip."

"I promised Constable George that I'd pop over to his office this morning to see if any of the results from the lab are back," Kerry reached for the cream and poured it into her mug until her coffee achieved the soft tan color promising a strong but sweet taste. "I hope to be back this afternoon to enjoy the sun on the dock."

"It's a shame you're leaving," Mrs. Kemp sat down in the chair next to Kerry. "You seem so at home here."

The comment took Kerry slightly by surprise since she had never spoken with Mrs. Kemp about where she was going or why. As far as Kerry knew, everyone just thought of her as a temporary guest with no attachment or interest in the small town.

"Lake Pines is definitely a beautiful town, I imagine it was a great place to raise a family."

A smile warmed Mrs. Kemp's face as she recalled flashes of her life, "It was."

Kerry ate while Mrs. Kemp reminisced about her years working and living in Lake Pines until they both realized an hour had passed and all the food was gone. Kerry stood and carried the empty dishes to the sink and thanked Mrs. Kemp before getting ready to leave for town.

Driving the boat was becoming second nature to Kerry, and she found she looked forward to the feel of the breeze and light mist that sprayed up as she drove toward town. The water was always slightly rougher on her way through Second Channel and she slowed the engine as she drove around the channel markers and early morning fishers that drifted in their boats around the opening, which Kerry learned was the ideal spot for them to catch fish.

The Main Street dock was empty and Kerry tied the boat up near the shore and walked the short distance to the police station where Peter had already been at work for a couple of hours.

He smiled when she walked through the door and Kerry felt excited about working on an investigation with Peter, renewing her love of her career. She just hoped the feeling would last when she arrived in Vancouver.

"I just received the results from the lab this morning," Peter reached for a sheet of paper that was sitting on the corner of his desk and handed it to Kerry. "The sand, as well as the pollen from the grass, are definitely from the beach on Wolf Island. The blood on the rock, as we suspected, is also a match for Velma's blood but tests weren't able to find any DNA from her attacker, which is unfortunate. But one thing is for certain, Velma was murdered on the beach at Half Moon Bay."

"What about the blue fibers that were hooked in her ring?"

"They were fluoropolymer fibers with a distinct dye used to achieve that particular shade of blue," Peter reached for another sheet with a blue square indicating the shade on a larger scale. "The hex number is 008ECC."

"Should that mean something to me?" Kerry asked although she did sense that the shade of blue was familiar and that she should be able to recognize it.

"It's the shade of blue used by several companies that supply teams that are involved in watersport activities."

"That makes sense since it's a waterproofed fiber, but I can't say that I recognize the shade. I was never involved in any watersports," Kerry drummed her fingers on the side of the desk.

"Think back to the day Velma's body appeared from under the dock," Peter prompted Kerry's memory.

Kerry snapped her head up when she realized where she had seen that particular shade of blue, "The club's sailing team?"

"The team jackets are white, with a slim red line over a large blue sleeve and front panel," Peter pointed to a poster advertising the race. "Just like that one."

Kerry thought back to meeting Byron Gray and the familiar jacket he was wearing on the day that he was preparing to start the race, as well as the look of shock when Velma's body floated out from under the dock.

"You know, Byron never let on that he knew that it was Velma Whitney who was in the water, and he obviously knew her very well," Kerry said. "It was like he was shocked to see her there."

"I called over to the club and Byron is there this morning setting up for a club tennis tournament and barbeque that's going on this afternoon," Peter grabbed his keys. "I'm going over to speak with him, do you want to come along?"

Kerry stood and nodded, "Definitely. He was a little too keen on pointing the finger of guilt toward Harrison now that I think of it."

As they walked down to the police boat docks Kerry asked Peter how Doctor Crampton had taken the news of her working alongside him on Velma Whitney's murder case. The voice inside her head told her she should step back from another coroner's case even though she knew he was wrong.

"At first he wasn't too happy, but eventually he dropped it and hasn't made a fuss. I'm not too sure how much longer he wants to stay working as the coroner," Peter pulled on the rope and unfastened the boat tie. "The job may be up for grabs soon if you're interested."

Kerry ignored the comment and sat in the seat next to Peter as he backed the boat out of the covered slip and headed toward Channel Island Summer Club.

Boats filled each slip on the docks as members arrived to take part in the club tennis tournament and barbeque. Glints of light bounced off the water and a group of cheerful women climbed out of a boat, their wide-brimmed hats shading their faces. The day was growing warm under the bright sun, and the clear blue sky and calm stillness in the air promised a perfect day for tennis. A young boy who helped them the last time they arrived at the club, ran toward their boat, grabbed the rope and pulled it toward his body. Within a few minutes, he had the front and back ropes secured to the dock and waved as he ran off to catch another boat and help the driver ashore.

When they reached the top of the steps, they could see Byron was in the center of a crowd of members who were receiving instructions and guidelines on the tournament. He finished his speech with the promise of a satisfying lunch afterward and everyone offered a round of applause for his effort in coordinating the festivities for the day. A bartender was making his way around the crowd, balancing a selection of glasses, some with ice water with lemon slices and others that looked to have a shade of lime margarita added to them. Byron saw Kerry and Peter standing on the deck when the crowd dispersed and walked over to them.

"Don't tell me you're here to join the tennis tournament? I'm the Activities Coordinator, I can probably squeeze you in," Byron let a small smile and laugh escape his otherwise conservative grin.

"No, we have a few questions concerning Velma Whitney, or specifically the day she died," Peter watched as Byron tensed and he pulled his arms across his chest.

"What exactly do you want to know?" His eyes darted toward fellow members who were glancing their way wondering why a Police Constable and a visiting coroner needed to speak with him.

"Where were you on the morning of the race?"

"I was at the Main Street dock," Byron pointed to Kerry. "You know that, I was with you when you found the body."

"I mean earlier in the day," Peter asked, narrowing the hours between four and six in the morning.

"I arrived at the club to collect the starters bag and flags at around six-thirty and then arrived at the Main Street dock close to seven to wait for the volunteers to arrive. Why?"

"We just want to make note of everyone's whereabouts on the day Mrs. Whitney was killed," Peter explained. "Do you remember seeing anything or anyone out of the ordinary that morning?"

Byron shook his head, "It was just a super busy race day morning. If you ask the staff in the kitchen they probably saw me getting my bags together before I left."

"I'll do that," Peter said, and Byron bristled at the notion of his whereabouts needing to be confirmed.

"Is that it? I have to get up to the courts to officially start the tournament."

"Just one more thing, could we get a look at the race jacket you were wearing on the morning of the regatta?"

"You can't, it was stolen out of my boat later that night. Sometimes people grab coats or fleeces from boats if they're

240

cold," Byron explained. "I'm sure it'll turn up."

"When it does, can you bring it to the station?"

Byron promised and after an awkward exchange of farewells, he ran up the stairs toward the tennis courts, disappearing behind a crowd of spectators. Kerry and Peter turned around to leave when the bartender stepped in front of them. He held the tray in front of Kerry and asked her if she wanted a drink, and she shook her head and thanked him.

"I think you may want to have a glass of water," the bartender's eyes widened and he pushed his eyebrows up high on his forehead and extended the tray once again.

Kerry grabbed a glass from the tray, and Peter did the same as the bartender spoke in a low whisper, "You're here because of Mrs. Whitney, right?"

Kerry nodded and took a sip of the water.

"Well, I don't know if it's important, but," and before he continued he looked to the side to make sure he couldn't be heard. "I overheard her arguing a few days before she was killed."

"Do you know who with?"

"I recognized Mr. Gray's voice and there was also a woman, but I couldn't tell you who it was, they were in the meeting room next to the kitchen. I heard them when I came in to prepare for the dinner crowd that night."

"What were they arguing about?"

"Mr. Gray was hoping to get a funding grant for the club to help pay for the tournaments he runs throughout the summer and when he didn't get it, he tried to have Mrs. Whitney approve the extra spending from the club's funds. But she refused and said she wasn't going to be bullied anymore into spending money the club didn't have."

"She used the word bullied?" Peter asked.

The bartender nodded, "Then Mr. Gray stormed out of the room and yelled that she'd regret turning him down."

They thanked the bartender and returned the two glasses to his tray and he slipped into the crowd of members offering cool drinks to those he passed.

"Byron Gray seems to be hiding the fact he had a problem with Velma, but maybe the mystery woman who was in the room will have more information about what happened, we just need to figure out who that was."

Peter turned and walked toward the club office, "I think I know exactly how to find out who that was."

19

The members' logbook was on a table next to the canteen registering each time someone arrived at the club and the purpose of their visit. Remarks varied from tennis, swimming, dinner, sailing and a few were noted as club meetings.

Two days before Velma Whitney was murdered there were many names written in the logbook. It was a warm day, and several members had arrived to use the courts or take out some of the club sailboats. Five were signed in for dinner and only two were signed in for a club meeting. Velma Whitney and Byron Gray.

"There's no mention of another person, the bartender said he also heard Velma arguing with a woman that night," Kerry flipped through the pages again, just in case she missed an entry.

"It doesn't mean they were arguing about the same thing," Peter suggested. "Maybe Mrs. Whitney had a separate argument with another member."

"I'm not sure how we can figure out who that was," Kerry looked around at the number of people coming and going from the club and all the boats that lined the docks in front of the club.

Peter ran his finger across the name of the member who had signed in for dinner with his family, "I know this man. His family always has a table for the annual hospital fundraiser. He was here while Mrs. Whitney was and maybe he saw something." Peter pointed to a couple sitting at a table on the deck. "That's him over there with his wife."

Kerry followed Peter out to the deck and to the couple who were enjoying a coffee at the only table covered by the shade of an oversized deck umbrella.

"Mr. and Mrs. Watson, how are you today?" Peter greeted the couple with a smile and received an instantaneous warm welcome. He introduced Kerry, and Mr. Watson invited them both to sit down, which they did.

"What brings you to the club today?" Mr. Watson asked, his rosy cheeks bright against his well-groomed silver hair and pale blue eyes.

"I'm looking into the death of Velma Whitney," Peter whispered, not wanting nearby teenagers to hear what he was talking about.

The faces on the friendly couple turned morose, "Such sad news about Velma. She'd done a lot for the club over the last number of years."

"The reason I wanted to speak with you is that two days before she died, she was overheard arguing with a woman. It was also the night you were both here for dinner with your family and I was wondering if you saw or heard anything."

"No, I'm sorry," Mr. Watson looked to his wife who also shook her head. "We were so excited to see our grandchildren that we really didn't stop to talk to anyone."

"That's too bad, but if you happen to remember anything, please give me a call," Peter pushed his chair back when Mrs. Watson spoke up with a suggestion.

Mrs. Watson's face lit up underneath her bright pink summer hat as she thought of a solution, "You could always check the security camera, it may have recorded who came and went that day."

Mr. Watson laughed and patted his wife's hand, "Lorna here has read every mystery novel printed, maybe she can help you."

"That's not a bad idea, Mr. Watson," Peter said and thanked the couple once more before heading to the office in search of the security camera recordings.

They went directly to Paul's office only to find it locked and the interior lights turned off.

"He's not here," the words came just before a series of bubble-gum snaps and a tilt of her head. "He left a little while ago to pick up some supplies in town, I think. But I'm not really sure."

The girl was dressed in clothing that was more in keeping with an afternoon in a skateboard park than a warm sunny day at an island summer club. Her black jeans, worn and faded, were snug to her thin frame and a heavy green hoodie floated around her body. Her hair was an unnatural shade of black and from the look of the teen's awkward stance, she had styled it into a ponytail on the recommendation of a parent and not by her choice.

"Is there any chance you have access to the security cameras?" Peter asked.

The young teenager, who was more interested in her latest social media posting than why Peter and Kerry wanted to see the security camera footage, pulled up the recording on her computer and left them in the office to watch it while she took a break.

They fast-forwarded through the morning and afternoon and watched as the evening brought a fresh wave of members to the club. The Watson's dinner party arrived, and they made note of every member who was captured walking under the glare of the camera, and they stopped when they saw Velma Whitney come into view. They rewound the footage and watched it again, slowing the speed to a regular pace. The camera captured two shadowy figures as they walked toward the corner of the deck where a lamp post was shining down a slim stream of light.

The film was grainy but the black and white image was clear enough that Kerry and Peter could see the two people who were arguing under the corner of the club building eave where the security camera was positioned. There was no sound and although Kerry couldn't read lips, she instinctively knew what the two women were arguing about. Their interaction was short but when Velma turned around and stormed off, the young blond was left standing alone under the single stream of light.

20

Braemar Island was only a few minutes from the club and they headed directly there once they were done watching the video footage. Peter decided to not call before he arrived. He knew if Harrison Whitney was hiding information about the day his wife was murdered, then he didn't want to allow him the time to think up another excuse or avoid more questions altogether.

It was Daniella Whitney who met them at the dock when their boat pulled up. It still amazed Kerry at how much she looked like her mother as she rushed up to grab their boat. She had been crying when they arrived, and Daniella wiped her cheeks with the back of her hand and forced a pleasant smile when Peter and Kerry jumped out of the boat. She mentioned how grateful she and her sister Helena were for their help in trying to figure out who had killed their mother and that they were in the process of planning an appropriate service that would not only honor their mother but allow them to give their mother's troubled life a peaceful end.

Daniella admitted that her mother's excessive drinking put pressure on relationships within their social circles but not to the point where she ever believed that someone would want to hurt her. Her lip quivered and tears rolled down her cheek as she pressed her lips together and shook her head. Kerry rested a hand on Daniella's shoulder and she took a deep breath and smiled.

"Sorry, it's still hard to talk about."

Daniella wiped away her tears and took Kerry and Peter to find her father. They walked along the same stone path that led to the front porch steps and then into the cottage, which this time, seemed to be even more disheveled than the last time they were inside.

Harrison jumped up from his chair when Daniella walked into the cottage with Peter and Kerry, and after his daughter left, he asked them why they were there.

"Did you find out who killed Velma?" Harrison slurred out the last syllable of his late wife's name.

They made the second visit to Braemar Island unannounced, and bottles that were previously hidden from view were now clearly displayed in cabinets. A glass of ice surrounded by clear pungent liquid and a suspended slice of lime, rested on the table next to Harrison Whitney's chair. The drink held the same distinct scent that Kerry recognized on his breath the first time she met Harrison, and although she couldn't immediately place it, it seemed strangely familiar.

"We've since learned that two days before your wife's murder that she had arguments with a couple of members from the club and we wanted to ask you about them."

Harrison, pleased with the prospect of the light of guilt being shone on someone other than himself, invited

Peter and Kerry to take a seat with him in the living room. He resumed his spot in his chair and wrapped his hand around the glass on the table and then quickly released his grip and folded his arms on his lap.

"What was it you found out?" He focused on each word as he spoke, a sign that it wasn't his first drink of the day. "You said she had some arguments?"

"Yes, one with Byron Gray, the Activities Coordinator at the club," Peter said. "Do you know him?"

Harrison sneered and rolled his eyes, "Yes, I know him. And he doesn't let anyone forget he's the Activities Coordinator of that club either. In fact, he rarely lets a conversation pass without mentioning it at least once."

Kerry thought back to each conversation that she had with Byron Gray and realized that although Harrison Whitney was being glib, he was also correct.

"I take it you're not a fan of his," Peter guessed Harrison's dislike of Byron Gray had less to do with his assertion of being Activities Coordinator and more to do with a personal reason.

Harrison could barely contain his laughter, "More like he was too much a fan of my wife. He's had a thing for her for years and he was less than pleased when she married me."

Peter smiled, but only slightly, at the fact he guessed correctly.

"Mr. Gray and your wife dated?" Kerry asked.

"Not really," Harrison took a sip of his drink and then licked his lips. "It was more of a one-way attraction. Byron had been trying to win over Velma's attention since she was old enough to date and she never returned his obsessive sentiments. He's only involved with the club because it ensures he can see her without me being around. He's more of a stalker than a friend."

"Did your wife have any problems with him?"

"Not that I know of, but he has been encouraging her to divorce me," Harrison shook his head. "Like it was any of his business."

"Were you and your wife having trouble in your marriage?" Kerry asked thinking back to the blond who was rubbing his back in the emergency room and who was also arguing with Velma two days before she was murdered.

Harrison was probably thinking of her too because his face suddenly bore a look of guilt, "We were working through a rough patch in our marriage, but we would've gotten through it."

"Byron mentioned your wife was thinking of selling the cottage, were you aware of that?" Peter's question caught Harrison off guard, and he wasn't prepared to conceal his shock.

"What are you talking about? She wasn't thinking of selling, she loved this place?" Harrison smashed his hand on the table and jabbed his wobbly finger in their direction. "Byron's just trying to cause trouble, it's him you should be looking at!"

Peter glanced over at Kerry who also registered the outburst at the mention of the sale of the cottage, one that didn't present itself when he was informed his wife was murdered.

"There was also someone else that your wife was seen arguing with that same day at the club, and we hoped that you could help us figure out who it was," Peter asked, moving the topic off of Byron Gray.

"I'll try," Harrison took a long gulp of his drink, still visibly upset at the mention of the sale of the cottage.

"We don't have a photo, but we saw them arguing on the security camera from the club," Peter waited until he could see Harrison's eyes until he finished his sentence. "It was the lady who was at the hospital with you yesterday."

"Hannah?" Harrison snapped. His hand jerked in shock and a small amount of liquid spilled over the edge of the glass. "There's no way they were arguing."

"Why would you say that?" Kerry asked. "It was obvious when we saw you at the hospital yesterday that you are both more than friends. Maybe your wife found out about the two of you?"

Harrison shook his head, "Impossible, things were never that serious with Hannah. We were just having some fun, it would've been over by the end of the week, she never sticks around with anyone for too long."

Harrison closed his eyes, regretting his wording and the nonchalant attitude he approached his marital unfaithfulness with.

"What I mean is that my fling with Hannah was just that – a fling," he stammered as he tried to explain. "It never would have interfered with my marriage."

"Maybe Hannah and your wife saw it differently," Kerry said, offering an alternate viewpoint, to which Harrison just offered a shrug.

"I think I'd like to speak with her myself if you don't mind," Peter interjected. "Can you give us her number?"

"I can't see why not," Harrison wrote Hannah's phone number on a piece of paper and handed it to Peter. "Her cottage is just around the corner on Hornby Island, it's the large blue one."

"That's the one right across from Half Moon Bay," Peter said, and then let a pause rest between them. "You don't think that's a bit of a coincidence?"

Harrison's blank face stared back at both Kerry and Peter, unsure of how to answer. "I guess I never thought of it."

Peter stood and walked toward the door, and then turned around just as his hand rested on the handle, "And don't call Hannah when we leave. If you do, you'll be charged with obstructing justice. Understand?"

Harrison nodded and didn't move from his seat. Kerry and Peter rushed down to the boat and headed to speak with Hannah, who was just across the bay from the scene of the crime.

21

Kerry squinted against the glare of the sun as it reflected off the chrome trim on the edge of the boat window. A row of cottages lined the perfectly sheltered bay on Hornby Island and today they were benefiting from the lack of clouds and wind, making it the perfect day to enjoy an afternoon on the dock.

There was only one blue cottage on the island, and it would have been impossible to miss both because of its size and position close to the water. Many of the cottages were set back double the distance, a measure, Peter explained to Kerry, that was put in place to protect the shoreline of the lake. Cottages and boathouses built before the restriction could build close to the shoreline. And because of the changes in regulations, many cottage owners fought their desire to upgrade or build a newer cottage since it would mean losing their vantage point close to the water.

Long swaths of green edged the property to the west of where the large blue cottage was built and cast a long skinny shadow across the lawn. Some of the deciduous trees had yet to come into full foliage, giving most of the island a desolate look from a distance. A large square dock extended off the side of a boathouse painted to match the cottage on land and stretched far enough out into the water to capture the sun, unimpeded by the shadows of the trees.

Blue and red umbrellas dotted the deck on the roof of the boathouse as well as the floating dock below. A boat was tied to the far side of the boathouse and two people were stretched out on lawn chairs.

It wasn't until they were closer, that Kerry recognized the two people on the dock. One was the woman Harrison was having an affair with, and who they came to speak with, and the other took them completely by surprise.

Peter's boat pulled up against the end of the dock just as Hannah wrapped her arms around the young man's neck. The deep rumbling sound of the engine eventually caught their attention and when they both saw the police boat, they pulled away from each other and Hannah turned down the music that was blasting from the speakers.

Kerry recognized the man immediately as the bartender who wasted no time in telling them that Velma was arguing with Byron two days before she was killed. Kerry found it odd that somehow he had failed to recognize the voice of the woman who had just been snuggling in his arms.

Hannah grabbed a towel from the chair and wrapped it around her body and then walked to the end of the dock and stood beside Peter's boat.

"Can I help you?" her face contorted as she looked back at the bartender who was pulling a shirt over his head.

Peter climbed up onto the dock and introduced himself, and Kerry followed behind, "I wanted to speak with you about a conversation you had with Velma Whitney two days before she died."

Hannah's eyebrows folded into a v-shape between her eyes, "What do you mean?"

"Your friend here told us he overheard two people arguing with Velma Whitney two days before she was killed. One was Byron Gray, and he has an alibi for the morning of the murder, and the other was you," Peter explained just as Hannah pulled back and began to deny knowing what he was talking about. "We saw you both on the security camera footage."

Hannah shot a stinging glare at the man standing behind her, "You what? Why would you say that, Alex?" She then turned to face Peter and Kerry who were waiting for an explanation.

"It was just a stupid argument, nothing huge," Hannah tightened her grip on her towel.

"Did she know about the affair you were having with her husband?" Peter asked.

Hannah hesitated for a while and then murmured that she wasn't sure, "I denied it since it wasn't a big deal. He's too old for me anyway. Harry was just fun to party with now and again."

Kerry noticed Alex's body shift and tense as Hannah referred to Harrison Whitney in a more than personal manner.

"And you can verify your whereabouts the morning of Velma Whitney's murder?"

"I was at the club with Alex," she pointed to the bartender standing behind her. "I spent the night there with him and we were together until everyone returned for the barbeque in the afternoon."

Alex began to nod his head rapidly as Peter and Kerry glanced his way.

Hannah pulled her arms around her body as she adjusted her towel, "That's when we heard about Velma's body floating out from under the dock at the start of the race."

Peter confirmed Hannah's alibi with Alex Berg, who they now knew was the club bartender as well as Hannah's on-again, off-again boyfriend.

Red patches began crawling up the sides of Alex's neck. Some people blushed easily when they were embarrassed, others reddened because it was impossible for them to hide a lie.

"What do you do at the club, Alex?" Kerry asked, taking both the bartender and Hannah by surprise, and his blush deepened.

"I'm the bartender at most of the functions, which is almost every second day, and I also do odd jobs and stuff around the club," Alex mumbled, almost as if he was embarrassed at his job requirements.

"What would some of the odd jobs and stuff be?" Kerry asked.

"I take care of small maintenance around the club, fixing loose boards, cutting the lawn, and I do all the supply runs into town as well."

"And today?" Peter asked.

"I had the afternoon off because I have to work a function that'll run late tonight," Alex explained.

"Did you ever have any contact with Velma Whitney during any of your routine duties at the club?"

Alex folded his arms across his chest and tucked his hands under his armpits and widened his stance, looking more relaxed and at ease than Hannah, who seemed to recoil and tense the longer Peter and Kerry remained on the dock.

"Mrs. Whitney had me help her with some inventory of the supplies I was picking up in town," Alex said.

"Why would she have you do that? Was that normal?" Peter asked.

Alex nodded, "She was responsible for paying the suppliers in town. She had me do it every Friday afternoon so she could work on the books and then make sure every bill was settled on Monday morning."

"Is there anything else?" Hannah asked. "We have a club dinner tonight and I have to get ready."

Peter looked to Kerry who then shook her head.

"No, but don't leave the area, either of you, I may have more questions for you both," Peter warned them before he climbed back into his boat.

Kerry jumped into the back of the boat and sat beside Peter and watched Alex and Hannah as they turned around and walked away. Hannah stomping several steps ahead of Alex. Kerry thought that Hannah wasn't looking forward to her dinner tonight, and in fact, Kerry sensed she looked a little panicky and afraid.

She wasn't sure if it was because Hannah was worried she'd be revealed as the killer or if it was because she knew who it might be.

22

The police sketch was surprisingly accurate. Josh Sutcliffe was still wearing the same black hoodie that he had on when he attacked Harrison Whitney in the parking lot and Kerry was impressed with the preciseness of both the artist and the store manager in the likeness they were able to achieve. Josh was twenty-four, had light brown hair, brown eyes, and a careless attitude. His arms were folded across his chest in a defiant pose and his body was slumped in the plastic chair he was sitting in.

The interrogation room was down the hall from Peter's office and Kerry listened from the next room while Peter questioned Josh and Officer Jones recorded their conversation.

A long scar ran along the right side of Josh's face, a souvenir he said, from the years before he ran away from home. Once he reached the age of sixteen, Josh decided that he no longer wanted to be a punching bag for his abusive stepfather and left to pursue a career as a musician.

The band, and his dreams, fell apart his second year in Sudbury when the band's singer signed a contract with a recording label in Toronto and left them all behind. Without a replacement for their lead singer, and no one interested in hiring a backup band, Josh was once again looking for work.

Part-time employment went only so far in paying the rent on the bachelor apartment he lived in, which was in the basement of a building that probably should've been condemned, and he picked up odd jobs around the lake to make ends meet. He found most of his lucrative employment during the summer months when cottagers were looking for repairs to docks, boathouses, and cottages.

Josh was leaving the Main Street docks when an officer spotted him. He instantly recognized the similarity to the sketch of Harrison Whitney's presumed attacker. He refused to answer any questions about the attack and had been sitting in the interrogation room by himself for almost an hour before Peter went in, not even asking to speak with a lawyer.

"Josh, we need to ask you some questions, and that's going to be difficult if you refuse to speak with us," Peter was frustrated but was able to keep his voice low and tone calm. "We can have a lawyer brought in for you if you'd like. It's your right."

"I know my rights," Josh blurted out. "I also know no matter what I say, I'm going to take the blame for what went down. It's always the same."

Peter didn't want to scare Josh from speaking, and he kept his next question simple, "What's always the same?"

Josh leaned forward and rested his arms on the table, "I'll end up taking the blame because I can't afford to get myself out of this." Josh lifted his arm and waved it over the table. "It's easier for you to pin this on a broke kid with no prospects."

"You're twenty-four, Josh, you're not a kid," Peter reminded him. "If you're found guilty, you'll be charged as an adult."

Josh looked down at his feet and sighed.

"What if I make a deal?" Josh asked, pleading with his eyes. "You do that sometimes don't you?"

"It depends on what you have to say."

Josh dropped his head into his hands, covering his face with his palms, "I never wanted to do it."

"Do what?" Peter asked.

"Hit on that rich guy and his girlfriend," Josh yelled. "But I couldn't turn down the money, it was too good.

And I only roughed him up and I never touched the girl, even though they wanted me to."

Peter realized that Harrison was not just some random target of a petty mugger, but the intended victim of the attack.

"Are you saying someone paid you to attack Harrison Whitney?"

Josh nodded.

"Who?"

Josh dragged his teeth across his lower lip, "Will you give me a deal and keep me out of prison?"

After some consideration, Peter promised to see that Josh receive only community service for his attack on Harrison Whitney, assuming the information he provided was legitimate. After Josh insisted Peter put their agreement in writing, he told them who hired him to attack Harrison Whitney. As Peter heard the name, he knew Kerry would be pacing outside the interrogation room door eager to start the conversation that Peter wasn't looking forward to having.

23

Daniella suddenly appeared to be much younger than her nineteen years as she sat in the brown vinyl chair waiting for Peter to call her into his office. Once Josh was certain he wouldn't be sent to prison for his attack on Harrison Whitney, he was more than eager to share the offer Daniella made to him the morning of the attack.

Five thousand dollars was a lot of money to most people, but especially to Josh since it amounted to over two months of backbreaking work on the lake. It would have been enough to let him enroll in the electrical apprenticeship program at Red River College, and hopefully, get him off the financial treadmill he'd been running on for the last several years.

Considering Josh had no prior charges for assault or aggressive behavior, Peter was inclined to offer Josh a chance to stay out of prison.

Daniella had met Josh when her mother hired him two summers ago to re-shingle their cottage and boathouse roofs. Daniella was immediately charmed by Josh's hard-luck story and impressed with the fact he'd been in a band and lived on his own. Neither Daniella nor Helena ever had to worry about where to live or how to pay bills, and she found Josh an easy friend to talk to over the years. The offer she made to Josh was made in the heat of her upset after finding out that her mother was murdered, and since she held her father responsible for the pain in her mother's life, she wanted to hit back. And Josh presented the opportunity to do that literally.

Daniella Whitney didn't try to deny paying Josh to attack her father and his girlfriend, and she broke down in tears when confronted with the reality that she almost ended Josh's freedom.

Everyone, especially Harrison Whitney, agreed that Josh would be best served if his involvement in the attack was kept out of the courts. As long as Josh would be spared from an arrest record, Harrison agreed he wouldn't press charges. Along with Josh's community service, Daniella was also going to have to perform volunteer service work for her part in the hired attack. However, Peter said it could wait until after Velma's funeral.

Cries of apology and anger at herself were met with tears from her father as he sat next to her.

When Kerry had first spoken with Daniella, something had passed between them. Kerry thought she had recognized the sense of loss and desperation in Daniella's eyes since she'd seen it once before. It was during a case in Montreal, when a young man lashed out at his sister's accused killer, stabbing him in the chest as he was leaving the courthouse. As Kerry watched Daniella fold under the grief of losing her mother in such a violent manner, and the pressure of the anger she pointed at her father, she wondered if there was something she could have done to prevent Daniella's actions.

In the end, there was nothing Kerry could have done, the only thing that would help anyone was to find out who murdered Velma Whitney. Then everyone could begin to heal.

24

It was after one in the morning by the time that the last guests left the club. He had been waiting in the backroom, pretending to have left the dinner with the rest of his friends. He doubled back, pretending to have forgotten something at the table, and was hiding ever since in the small locked closet, siphoning courage from his bottle of gin.

Alex still had another hour left to clean and close the bar before he could leave for the night. He watched through the small keyhole as Alex removed the last of the dishes and glasses from the tables.

The volume on the stereo suddenly exploded and Alex sang along with a heavy metal band that was screeching through the speakers.

He was hiding in wait only because Alex had stumbled upon what he had done, but he still wasn't sure the dopey bartender even knew what he had found. But it was clear from what he overheard Alex telling Velma that Alex was going to make sure he shielded himself from any blame. The only reason Alex was even hired was that no one else had applied for the position.

If it had been up to him, he would've hired one of the member's kids and paid them cash under the table. Unfortunately, the club needed someone old enough to serve alcohol and strong enough to pick up their deliveries in town. And none of the kids applying for jobs could satisfy those requirements and now he was faced with stopping Alex before he could reveal to the committee what he had done.

He dashed out from where he was hiding when he heard the final clanging of the dishes in the kitchen. Moving as quietly as he could, he made it down to the dock and jumped into the back of the club boat that Alex had been using since the beginning of the summer. It was an old fishing boat, with rusted seams along the hull and deep enough to hold the boxes of supplies Alex collected weekly, and sturdy enough for an inexperienced boater.

His head was spinning, and his heart pounded against his ribs. He pulled his knees up to his chest, bit his lip, and tried to summon the courage he found in the closet with the gin. It was what was going to give him the strength to do what he needed to do, but as he breathed in the damp mold scent of the boat's tarp, his stomach twisted.

He exhaled, emptying his lungs and holding his diaphragm down. Now wasn't the time to be sick.

The morning with Velma was much more disturbing. Taking care of Alex shouldn't be as difficult since he held no attachment to the kid, and he had time to plan his attack.

It would look like a mugging and he'd do it in the back alley near his building. He had already checked out the area the night before and very few windows looked out onto the lane, and with the right move to cover Alex's mouth first, he'd be sure to muffle his yells. He envisioned how the attack would unfold, now he just had to wait for Alex to come down from the club.

His pulse quickened when he heard footsteps pounding down the wooden steps of the club, followed by a thud on the bottom of the boat. The engine vibrated, startling him, and then his body rolled back as the boat pulled away from the dock.

Each move of the boat jarred his stomach and rattled his head, but he knew if he could just make it to shore without Alex knowing he was behind him, then he'd be able to do what he needed to do without being seen.

Finally, the boat slowed down and then the engine stopped. Alex was still singing that stupid song he had blaring at the club and it was an odd thought to think it would be the last song he'd sing.

Guilt and pain briefly gripped him, but he pushed the feeling aside when he remembered what he had already done and what he'd risked keeping Velma from revealing his secret.

Slowly and quietly, he lifted the tarp and watched Alex as he climbed out of the boat and then onto the dock. He waited until he was far enough away and then he followed along the same path, shielding himself in the shadows as he ran.

The gin had taken hold, and he became braver the closer he came to Alex and when he was near enough, he reached out and wrapped his arm around Alex's neck and covered his mouth.

He wasn't prepared for Alex to jerk back his right leg and kick his knee. The move caught him off balance and his grip loosened from around Alex's neck, and he was suddenly free from his grip. He ran after him and pounced on Alex's back, pulling on his shoulders and dragging him to the ground. Short nervous stabs followed each scream, and he felt like he was going to be sick. The feeling the knife made as it sliced Alex's skin and as it tore into his muscles differed greatly from when he used the knife to cut the rope on a sail.

His palm felt tacky against the metal of the small rigging knife, clinging to his sweaty palm. Alex pushed against the attack, and the force of each shove drove his head against the pavement. As Alex fell silent, the deafening throb of his pounding pulse resounded in his ears and his deep labored breathing filled the space around them.

By the time anyone found him, he will have bled out, and he'd certainly be dead by then. He'd return to Channel Island and leave the club boat in the slip near the shed, and change his clothes before getting into his own boat and returning to his cottage.

With his boat lights turned off, he was sure no one would see him as he drifted into the bay by his cottage, and then maybe by morning, he could put the two murders behind him.

With each move of a wave, queasiness overtook him and he leaned over the side of the boat. Finally giving up the fight against the nausea that stabbed at his gut, which he thought, was easier to feel than the guilt.

25

The call to the club president, Paul Jensen, was quick and fruitful. Within ten minutes he had emailed a list of members who had purchased the sailing team jacket over the last two years. The team had updated their design and adopted the recent shade of blue after a member wanted their design to match the Olympic team colors hoping it would spark a winning attitude and record. The team of thirty placed their orders, eager to be ready for their summer race season. Peter was able to rule out eighteen of the members who still hadn't arrived for the summer, leaving a dozen jackets to track down. The elusive jacket, of course, being Byron Gray's which was mysteriously removed from his boat.

Officer Jones was assigned the tedious duty of tracking down the jackets, while Kerry and Peter drove to the cottages to collect them. They gathered each jacket and returned to the lab where Kerry examined each one under a high-powered microscope for scratches or pulls in the fabric.

"This coat's fabric is a definite match for the fiber found in Velma Whitney's ring," Kerry determined. "However, none of the jackets we collected show any signs of being the one worn by the killer. Outside of the odd spot of mold or food stains on some jackets, there is no evidence that Velma Whitney's attacker had worn any of them."

"We've accounted for every jacket," Peter crossed the last name off the list. "I'm not sure where to look now."

Kerry leaned her back against the examination table and crossed her arms, "That just leaves Byron Gray's jacket."

Peter closed his eyes and stretched his neck to the left and right and let out a deep sigh. "We need to speak with Byron one more time before we can rule him out as a suspect."

Byron answered his phone on the second ring, and after some slight hesitation, he agreed to cancel his meeting to speak with Peter that afternoon.

A half-hour later, Kerry and Peter were pulling into the small rocky bay in front of Byron's cottage.

Late day shadows crawled across the dock, shading the bay and the front of Byron's cottage. There was a slight lean to the building, and the entire north side of the structure was marked with mold. The small cabin sat on the center of the property, which was nestled between two larger, and much more modern cottages on Brickstone Island. Peter wasn't sure where, or how, the island received its odd moniker. Most people believed the name was a result of a misprint at the land titles office, and that the intended name was Blackstone Island, which referenced the color of the rock that covered the land.

Buyers and property assessors valued lake properties according to some simple features. Accessibility, sun exposure, and water quality.

Of the three features that apparently deemed the value of Lake Pines cottage property, Byron Gray's wouldn't have ranked very high on any list. Rough low water and sunken logs that were remnants of past log booms that drifted near the island, hampered access to the small rocky island. And even though Byron's cottage was in the center of the island, high trees and tall neighboring cottages shaded his building that overlooked an already darker northern facing bay. Large rocks and tall reeds littered the bay, the latter which unfortunately for Byron, were illegal to dredge and remove, leaving the water uninviting for swimmers.

Despite the worn-down state of Byron's cottage, the wide porch that stretched across the entire width of the dark brown building seemed oddly welcoming. Two chairs angled for conversation with a small wrought-iron table between them, and an antique butter churn stuffed with white and fuchsia shade-loving impatiens, made the cottage looked more inviting close up than from the water.

Through the window, Kerry could see Byron as he sat quietly staring at some pages in his hand. His shoulders slumped forward and the outer edges of his tear-filled eyes sagged. He looked pensive, sad, and alone.

Peter knocked on the door and Byron jumped slightly in his chair and then hurried through his small living room to answer the door. Kerry watched him through the window as he moved from his chair to the door, with some difficulty and a slight limp in his leg.

Byron pulled open the door and invited them inside with a small, uneasy smile. He was wearing a bright orange loose-fitting shirt and brown pants that were too small. He seemed oddly suited as a realtor, both in the state of his cottage and the clothing he was wearing.

"Thank you for delaying your meeting," Peter said as he took a seat in the long sofa pushed up under the front window. Kerry sat across from Peter and in the chair next to Byron.

A worried look of concern crossed Byron's face, and he bit down on his lower lip.

"It's been completely distracting, to be honest, having you come back to me again regarding Velma's murder," Byron was nervously rubbing his hands together, turning the skin on his knuckles a deep red.

"Well, we've had a bit of a problem nailing down your whereabouts the morning of the murder," Peter explained.

"I told you I was at the club getting my bags and then I went straight to the Main Street dock to set up for the race," Byron said, a little more firmly than necessary. "Didn't you speak with the kitchen staff at the club?"

"I did, and they don't remember seeing you arrive that morning, and the security cameras don't angle to the dock so if you were there, we didn't see you. Plus, we have no way of confirming the time you arrived at the Main Street dock either," Peter waited for Byron to defend himself or come up with another excuse, but instead, he turned his head away as tears filled his eyes. Kerry grabbed the carton of tissue and held it out for Byron, and he pulled two from the box.

"I cared about Velma," he wiped his raw hand over his eyes, smudging the tears on his cheeks and soaking the tissues. "I never would've hurt her!"

Peter opened the file folder on his lap and pulled out the magnified image of the blue fiber Kerry pulled out of the clasp of Velma's ring, "We found this blue fiber in the clasp of Velma's wedding ring and we believe it belonged to the killer. It's an exact match for the material used for the sailing team jackets, and yours is the only one we haven't been able to examine."

Color drained from Byron's face as he stared at the page, "I didn't do it, I don't know what else I can say to make you believe me. My coat was stolen from my boat, but if you find it, there won't be a rip on it because I was wearing it that morning and I definitely didn't kill Velma!"

The anxiousness in his voice would've been difficult for most people to fake and his shoulders trembled, even though there wasn't a chill in the room. Byron Gray was angry, and it was anger that killed Velma Whitney but was it *his* anger specifically that was responsible for her murder?

Kerry looked past Byron's head and to the shelf of books and photographs that lined the wall.

"There are a lot of photos you've collected over the years," Kerry pointed to several of them where she recognized the front of the club.

Byron twisted his body and smiled when his eyes rested on some photos where he and Velma were standing next to each other. A question settled beneath his awkward smile.

"What do you think happened to her?" Byron asked, but didn't avert his eyes from the images of Velma. "She never hurt anyone."

Kerry scanned the photos and a quick count left her with close to twenty that contained Byron and Velma, standing together and smiling. Peter asked Byron again to think of anyone who could account for his whereabouts on the morning of Velma's murder.

Byron looked down to his knees as he replayed the morning in his mind and then his face shot up when he remembered something, "I stopped for gas before I arrived at the Main Street dock and Mrs. Huntley was there getting some drinks for the volunteers."

Peter wrote the name and phone number of the gas attendant as well as Mrs. Huntley and said he would contact them later to confirm his story.

The colorful photographs caught Peter's eye, and he was about to ask Byron about Harrison's suggestion that he was more of a stalker than a friend to

Velma when his phone rang. The officer on the other end of the line was calling from the hospital and urgently trying to contact him on behalf of a patient.

Peter listened and then said he'd be on his way and ended the call.

"We need to leave now Mr. Gray," Peter stood and closed the folder shut. "I'll contact you if we need any further information."

Kerry followed Peter to the front door and turned to Byron, "I hope we didn't have you miss an important meeting?"

Byron brushed his hand in the air and smiled, "Heath wanted to meet with me and the other committee members about needing to find a new treasurer, and I wasn't looking forward to doing that. Velma's death seems so raw. I'm waiting for her to storm through the doors and ask why we're not working!" A smile crossed Byron's teary face.

They left Byron in the cottage and Kerry was certain she heard him cry the moment the door closed.

Kerry followed Peter down the path and then along the dock and waited for him to explain the call he received and why they needed to rush out of Byron Gray's cottage.

"Alex Berg was viciously attacked last night and since he was on the list of people we spoke with, Officer Jones thought we may want to know," Peter turned the key in the ignition and the engine rumbled and the dark water churned below the boat. "I'm going to go over and speak with him now. I can drop you off at the dock before I go to the hospital."

Kerry dropped into the seat beside Peter, "I'm coming too."

There was one spot left on the hospital dock and Peter pulled the police boat into the slip and secured the ropes. They arrived in Alex's examination room just as the doctor was about to suture his wounds when Peter asked him to stop. Perplexed, the doctor stepped away from Alex when Peter promised it would only be a moment.

"I'll come back in ten minutes, after that, the freezing will have worn off," the doctor pulled off his protective gloves and tossed them in the garbage, and then left the room uttering a small huff.

"What happened Alex?" Peter asked.

"Last night I was on my way home after the club dinner and out of nowhere some guy jumped me," Alex explained.

"My neighbor found me this morning. I was out cold and covered in blood and she freaked out and called the ambulance."

"Did you get a look at the guy who jumped you?" Peter asked as Kerry flipped the pages in his hospital file.

"No, but he was strong and a little taller than I am because when he grabbed me from behind his arm fit around my neck easily," Alex squirmed at the pain in the back of his shoulder. "I took a lot of stab wounds in my back before he eventually hit me over the head."

Peter made a few notes in his book.

"I don't remember anything else," Alex's voice trembled.

"Can I take a look?" Kerry pointed to Alex's back.

Alex nodded and Kerry helped him lean forward and she examined the wounds that the doctor was about to suture closed. The cuts were deep and ragged, and Alex curled his toes at the slightest touch. Local anesthetic was starting to lose its effectiveness and Kerry could see beads of sweat form on Alex's temple.

"Did you see what your attacker stabbed you with?" Kerry helped Alex lean back on the pillow.

"Whatever it was, it was shiny, because it reflected the light in the back lane," Alex's face winced at the pain that shot through his back as Kerry lowered him onto a pillow.

The doctor returned to the room and insisted on stitching up Alex's wounds.

"If you think of anything else, Alex, call me," Peter said. "And get well soon, okay?"

Alex smiled and thanked them for rushing over and promised to contact them the instant he remembered anything and even joked he was glad to have a couple of days off work. Kerry followed Peter out of the room and closed the door behind them when they were in the hall.

"Whatever was used to stab Alex had a short blade with a serrated edge," Kerry said.

"Like a switchblade?" Peter asked.

Kerry twisted the side of her mouth and shook her head, "Short like that, but it was probably curved and definitely had a row of teeth on one side."

Peter and Kerry left the hospital room with more questions than answers and knew that whoever killed Velma had some connection to Alex, they just needed to find out what it was. But one thing was for certain, their questions were bringing them closer to the murderer.

26

It was late when Kerry returned to Fox Lodge, the sun had just dropped below the horizon an hour earlier, and the familiar sounds of darkness were beginning to fill the air. The melodic harmony of the frogs that resided in the base of the reeds near the shore mixed with the cricket's cry, that usually lulled her to sleep, welcomed her arrival. Mrs. Kemp was reading in the large living room, waiting for Kerry to return, and a soft light poured from the windows of the lodge illuminating the edge of the path. The lodge was inviting and Kerry hurried up the front lawn, immediately struck with the sweet scent of the night air that was reminiscent of an approaching storm.

Fresh field growth brushed the edge of her shoe, making a swishing sound as she walked up the path, low-lying moss and lily-of-the-valley poked through the ground returning life to the island.

Thunder rumbled a deep throaty warning and Kerry could swear that she could feel the electricity in the air. Yellow squares of light folded onto the lawn, spilling out of the cabin's windows and Kerry could see Mrs. Kemp's silhouette as she read in a large green chair. The squeaky hinge startled Mrs. Kemp as Kerry pulled the old wooden door open and stepped inside.

She stood from her overstuffed chair, folded her book closed, placed it on the table, and welcomed Kerry back with a small hug.

"I kept some dinner warm for you," Mrs. Kemp sprinted ahead of Kerry and prepared the roasted chicken and potatoes on the plate that was being kept warm in the oven.

"You didn't have to do that," but as the words left Kerry's mouth, her stomach growled. She hadn't eaten much that day, except for a muffin and coffee midday to try to quell her appetite, which hadn't quite succeeded.

Kerry ate the meal and filled Mrs. Kemp in on their investigation, leaving out her suspicions she had about Byron Gray. As Mrs. Kemp listened, Kerry realized how much she missed being involved in work. It had been over half a year since she left Montreal and the last few days her memories of the city, her job, and of Jean flooded back into her mind. Her old boss, and dear friend, had made her promise to stay in touch and to contact him every week to let him know she was alright. She had done neither.

Her attempt at avoidance did little to keep her mind from returning to her old life once she became involved in helping Peter with Velma Whitney's murder, and seeing Doctor Crampton in a job similar to hers, but lacking the energy or interest to fulfill his obligations, was becoming difficult.

After dinner, Mrs. Kemp grabbed two small glasses and a bottle that was tucked in the back of a cupboard above the sink and invited Kerry to share a drink on the dock.

Kerry followed Mrs. Kemp down to the dock and she gazed above, tilting her head back to take in the thick velvet of midnight blue that stretched across the sky holding the stars in place. At the same time that the darkness gave the sensation of being wrapped tight, the island and lake seemed to open up to the vastness of the sky above.

The angle of the two Adirondack chairs invited their company, looking out into the bay and the wide stretch of water. Mrs. Kemp poured two glasses of clear liquid and handed one to Kerry.

"I think it's a good thing that you're working with Peter on this case," Mrs. Kemp smiled as she spoke. "He's always been driven to solve every case that comes across his desk, and I just don't think that Doctor Crampton is up to the task anymore."

"Do you think it's time for him to retire?" Kerry asked, realizing it was really none of her business, especially since she was planning on leaving Lake Pines.

Mrs. Kemp lifted her hand to her face and brushed away the hair that blew across her eyes, "I don't know that he has the energy to keep up with Peter, and considering what happened to his father, he doesn't stop until he solves each case."

"What happened?" The question left Kerry's lips before she even considered if she really wanted to know. Often, being aware of a co-worker's past made it more difficult to work with them because it ended up being all she thought about.

"When Peter was a little boy, maybe around ten years old, his father was killed when he was fishing at night," Mrs. Kemp closed her eyes and shook her head as she explained the traumatic accident that devastated Peter's family. "He was one of my students that year and I saw how it devastated his family. His mother was so young and left with a small family to raise. She had a lot of support from friends and people in the community, but it wasn't the same."

"Was the boater ever caught?"

"No, and it's what pushes Peter to ensure that every case gets solved, no matter how hard he has to work."

They let the silence settle between them and they both gazed over the water in the bay and watched thin shards of moonlight bounce of the rippling water, lulling them both into a sleepy trance.

"This is one of my favorite times of the year," Mrs. Kemp spoke in a whisper. "Before the summer fully awakens and ahead of when most cottagers arrive. It's peaceful and calm. Eventually, the noise of the boat engines will carry across the bay, even at night, and the town will be overrun with tourists."

"That's a good thing, though, isn't it?" Kerry asked.

"Oh, yes," Mrs. Kemp laughed. "But for a little while, we get to keep Lake Pines all to ourselves."

Kerry clinked glasses with Mrs. Kemp and agreed that the peacefulness was unique, and although she hadn't experienced a summer in Lake Pines, she could understand the desire to huddle around the calmness while it lasted.

The scent from the glass overtook Kerry as she sipped the drink and it reminded her of the smell that came from the glass that Harrison Whitney was drinking from.

"What is this?"

"Lavender gin," Mrs. Kemp said and then lifted the glass to her nose and took a deep breath. "It was a gift Simon received from one of the cottagers."

"I don't ever remember tasting anything like this."

"Oh, I'm not surprised," Mrs. Kemp smiled. "It's made in small batches by one of the cottagers. He gave Simon a few bottles after Simon took a few men out for a guided fishing tour. This is our last bottle."

"Who makes it?"

Mrs. Kemp shrugged her shoulders, "Not sure. I never asked Simon."

Their conversation ended there, both feeling tired and relaxed under the night sky. The rumbling storm, muted in the distance, had yet to roll into Lake Pines and block the stars from view, and the light breeze picked up to a warm gentle wind.

The taste of the lavender gin was sweet on Kerry's tongue and the combination of the calming scent and second glass relaxed her shoulders. She leaned back in the chair and looked up at the night sky, flooded with stars, and at that instant, she felt like she could reach out and touch one. The sky seemed closer in Lake Pines, unimpeded by skyscrapers or towers, making the continuous curve stretch from one end of the lake to the next.

And she could see it all. And for a brief moment, she felt like there was nowhere else in the world.

Mrs. Kemp stood, stretched her arms above her head, and walked back to the lodge, ready to turn in for the evening. When Kerry looked back, Mrs. Kemp was still standing on the porch looking up at the sky.

Kerry returned her attention to the light lapping sounds of the water and the soft breeze that brushed against her face and offered Mrs. Kemp some privacy.

Her thoughts returned to their conversation about Peter. What she had learned about him shouldn't have changed what she felt about him as a police officer, but it did. His chosen profession made sense, as did his drive to ensure that every victim finds peace.

For their memory as well as their family's ability to move forward.

Peter and his family didn't receive that sense of peace when his father died and that haunting pain needled him forward, making sure that no case went unsolved.

There was no question now. Kerry had to stay in Lake Pines and help Peter find the evidence necessary that would reveal the killer. The answers, she knew, lay with the victim, hidden in the evidence left on her body or at the scene of the crime, and no matter how dangerous it seemed, she needed to help find the clues that Peter may not see.

Like most danger, it seeped in from areas and spaces that you couldn't easily see, and she wondered if the same held true for Velma Whitney's murder.

Kerry spent the remaining hour sitting on the dock, staring up at the sky in complete silence. The distant cry of a loon echoed over the lake, its shrill reverberating off the night air, sending a chill up Kerry's spine. Not because of fear, but because of a deep emotional rush that swept over her.

The buzz of the text coming through Kerry's phone pierced the silence of the perfect evening. She pulled it out of her pocket and the blue light lit up her face on the end of the long dark dock as she read the text from Jean.

He had been on a conference call with an associate of his in Vancouver and he'd learned that he was looking to fill a vacant coroner's position. Jean had informed his associate, Doctor Burton, that Kerry was relocating to Vancouver and that she'd be a perfect fit.

Doctor Burton was so impressed with Jean's effusive recommendation of Kerry that he was interested in speaking with her.

But there was one catch. Doctor Burton was being pressured by the city to fill the position, and she needed to let him know if she was interested as soon as possible.

27

Helena was the first to suggest the theme for their mother's funeral service and Daniella happily agreed. It was, after all, her favorite activity when she was at the lake. Her lawyer had read the Will over the phone to only Daniella and Helena. They arranged the private call after they informed their mother's lawyer about the suspicions the Lake Pines police had against their father.

Mr. Crosby, who had never liked Harrison, eagerly agreed to extend several leniencies to the girls where their mother's Will was concerned. He'd been the one to inform Harrison that Velma had changed her Will and that he wouldn't receive the lump sum payment nor the hefty annuity that was promised to him.

In the lawyer's mind, both his infidelities and the shadow of guilt in her murder were reasons enough to bar him from collecting any money from his wife's inheritance. But in the end, it was the fine print in her Will that gave him the legal backing he required.

Everything, in the end, would go to Daniella and Helena and he would be asked to step aside from any plans for her funeral.

Their father reacted to being excluded from their plans in anger. Daniella wasn't sure if it was because of the loss of money or that both of his daughters believed he could be guilty of murdering their mother.

He begged his daughters to believe he was innocent and that he loved Velma. Harrison assured them both that no matter what evidence the police had, that they were wrong. Helena cried as Harrison grabbed her shoulder and begged her to forgive him, and she ran away when he promised to spend the rest of his life trying to make it up to her.

The money didn't matter, he claimed, and he only wanted a relationship with them.

Daniella pushed aside the envelope that arrived from Mr. Crosby, delivered by courier to a lawyer in Lake Pines. It contained the completed documents that confirmed their father's accounts had been closed and he no longer had access to any of their mother's funds.

Helena wondered if they had made a mistake and if their father deserved more consideration. Daniella slammed her hand on the table, reminding her sister of the years stolen because of their father's affairs.

The last thing they had to do before the funeral was to call Mary and make sure she was here to spread their mother's ashes as she had stipulated in her Will. The place where their mother wanted her ashes spread was difficult for Daniella and Helena since it was also the island where she was killed.

Mary had convinced them that no matter how painful it would be, or how odd it would seem, that it was what Velma would have wanted. Mary promised them both that Velma had many more years of joy on Wolf Island and that they couldn't let a few minutes of pain take away all that was special for Velma.

They would wait for Mary to arrive and then the three of them would follow Velma's wishes at her favorite spot. They would go out to Wolf Island, climb the steep rocky cliff until they reached the peak at the top, and with only the air to carry her, their mother would be free. And there was nothing their father could do to stop them.

28

He had one chance to make this work since he had already failed at keeping the police from asking questions. He was angry with himself for not being able to control his anger and for not doing a better job at planning on how to approach Velma. An argument was expected, but as he thought back to the bloodied rock, he slammed his hand on the steering wheel and swore. Every time that night rushed back to him, his neck muscles tensed and his breathing quickened.

Hiring an investigator was beyond what he thought she would ever resort to and he never imagined that she would be as vindictive as she was when she found out what happened.

After all, they were friends their entire life, or at least as far back as he could remember. He held none of the poor decisions she made against her, and unlike some of her friends, he never brought up the 'remember when' stories that they often did.

Sobriety was important to Velma and even though he wasn't interested in diving headfirst into that lifestyle, he still gave her the breadth and respect to do what she needed to do.

He still had nightmares of that morning on Half Moon Bay when he confronted Velma. She threatened to reveal what he had done no matter how intently he pleaded. She'd warned him that she would tell everyone after the race, and every plea he made went ignored.

It was a process of making things right, she had explained. As if it would make the sting of what she was about to do less painful.

Uncovering his secrets was one thing, bringing them to light knowing what would happen to him was another. It would hurt so many people, and ruin him in the process.

He could recall everything about that morning, unable to push each scene from his mind. He'd waited near her cottage and followed her as she drove to Half Moon Bay on the morning of the regatta. He expected her to go directly to the club and had planned on stopping her before she reached the dock, but when her boat veered to the left, he continued to follow her.

Trailing Velma wasn't a regular occurrence, and he didn't realize she still used the island for climbing, as she and her friend Mary often did when they were younger. He would see them scaling to the top of the island and then they would sit there for hours talking and avoiding the group of them on the beach. He just chalked it up to her shyness and never imagined it was because she didn't like them.

Now, he wasn't sure.

Over the last couple of days, the fright that woke him in the middle of the night wasn't the memory of the final blow of the rock against her skull, but the first moment he put his hand on her arm. He didn't mean to knock her off her climb, but when she fell against the sand, her shock caused her to scream and try to run.

The fog and thick mist were beneficial to offering him a shield from any boats passing through the bay, but he knew from his years on the lake that her screams would easily carry through the stagnant morning air. Echoing through the stillness and rebounding off the curved rock apex on the island.

He'd heard the eagles when they first nested on the island years ago and realized how easily even the minutest of sound carried over the calm dead of the lake.

Putting his hand over her mouth was meant to calm her, but he could see now that his quick move made her want to fight back. He pleaded and begged for her to reconsider. He asked her to think about all the people she would hurt, but she refused to change her mind. She said that she needed to be focused on making things right, in order to regain her own strength.

He didn't even remember reaching for the rock or lifting it above his head. And the motion in between when he brought his arm down on her head was a blur. That's when he panicked.

He tossed the rock into the thick clump of grass and shook her shoulders. Her head slumped to the side and fell back into the sand as he tried to lift her up.

It was the amount of blood that surprised him the most. It had splattered across her face and into the sand where she lay. His jacket was spotted red, stark against the white and blue fabric.

With no cover on the island and the cover of fog lifting, there was only one thing he could do. Shielding himself from guilt would only be possible if he wasn't caught. In addition to hiding his crime, he now had to hide Velma's body.

The bay was the only place he could go. He pulled her body into the water, pushed her under the surface, and dragged her past the protection of the rocks. It took three tries and then he finally pushed her into the open current.

Once he could no longer see Velma's body, he returned to the spot on the beach where he had killed her and scooped the blood-soaked sand, and dumped it into the water. Velma's blood and any sign of the crime that was committed quickly sank to the bottom.

Velma's scarf had come loose from her neck as he dragged her along the sand and had blown into the stalks of grass. He shoved it into his pocket and pushed his boat off the beach and headed home.

He didn't expect the lake to pull her toward the Main Street dock or that she'd appear from under the slip just as the regatta was about to start.

How could he? He didn't plan the murder, and if he had, it wouldn't have played out so violently or aggressively.

This time, he made sure that he wouldn't be caught. He would be in and out of the cottage before anyone even knew he was there. While at the club, he overheard Helena mentioning that Harrison insisted on taking an overnight boat trip to Sweeny's Fishing Lodge where the three of them could plan a proper service for Velma. It was the perfect time to look for the documents that Velma had threatened him with, and the reason that their argument culminated in her death. Something that didn't need to happen.

He arrived at the cottage after midnight, late enough that he knew most people on the lake would be asleep and it would be less likely he'd be seen. Like most cottages, theirs was unlocked, and he entered easily and without notice. A brown sweater and yellow raincoat hung on the hooks next to the door and the jacket wouldn't look out of place. The empty room held Velma's memory alive with photos and scents, and he momentarily thought about changing his mind when he remembered what Velma said and what he was trying to protect.

The bedrooms were upstairs, above the life and routine of the Whitney family, and would be an ideal hiding place. Assuming Velma wasn't lying about the evidence she had against him. His heart pounded with each step that he took. The solid oak banister rose to the second floor of the cottage in three sections. A window ran the entire length of each floor, the one oddity in the cottage built at the turn of the century when small windows were the norm. The light from the moon crept across the lawn and long thin shadows from the birch grove clawed at the lawn. He paused at the top of the last step, took a deep breath, and ran his shaking fingers through his hair.

The hall was long and dark, and each step he made creaked under his feet. The door was ajar and he could easily make his way around the room guided only by the light of the moon. It was easy to distinguish which side of the bed Velma slept on. A small blue glass vase, a John Le Carré novel with a page dogeared three-quarters of the way through, and a small silver frame with a picture of Daniella and Helena sat atop one night table. A glass and a wallet on the other.

He pulled open drawers and pushed his hand under piles of cotton and silk clothing, feeling for hidden paper or files underneath. He fanned the pages of her novel, opened her night table drawer, and lifted her mattress.

Nothing.

He continued his search in that room and the others in the cottage until he finally had to admit that whatever she was hiding wasn't there. Momentarily he wondered if she was bluffing and if he had killed her for nothing. He dragged the back of his hand across his brow and sighed.

It was past two in the morning and he knew he had exhausted his search, and no matter how much he hated to admit it, it was time to leave.

The voice behind him came as a complete surprise as did the angry face of Harrison as he caught him closing the cupboards in their bedroom closet. Harrison charged at him, shouting accusations and threats.

Harrison wasn't as tall as he was, but what he lacked in height, he possessed in fierceness. He never liked Harrison, but he never knew him to be an idiot either. Within moments of pulling him away from Velma's chest of drawers, Harrison knew that whatever he was looking for was also the reason his wife was killed.

"I can't believe you killed her!" Harrison shouted, tears fresh in his eyes and the sour smell on his breath as he slurred his words. "What could she have done to you!"

Their arms were entwined as Harrison tried to pull him out of the room and he threatened to call the police. Harrison jerked his wrist free after a failed attempt at a punch, and instead of charging at him again in his drunken rage, he pulled his phone out of his pocket and dialed the number he had stored in his phone for Constable George.

He ran at Harrison without thinking of what his next move was and they tumbled out of the bedroom, into the hall and their backs were against the thick oak banister as Harrison tried to push him away.

Harrison's phone fell out of his grip and somersaulted over the banister and bounced onto the first landing, shattering the screen.

He had come to find the documents that would destroy his life when he thought no one was there. Instead, he watched as the flailing body of Harrison Whitney crashed through the banister and landed on the floor below them, plummeting down with a scream trailing behind him.

Eventually, all he could hear was his own heavy breathing as Harrison fell silent in a twisted form at the bottom of the stairs. Neither Daniella nor Helena came running which meant they weren't in the cottage and still had a chance to escape. He ran down the stairs, averting his eyes from Harrison's twisted form, and opened the front door of the cottage. He walked beneath the shadow of the trees and then drifted his boat out of the bay before starting the engine.

A rumble of thunder echoed off in the distance and contrasted the clear star-filled sky above him. He took the longer route home, and to avoid the nightmares that plagued him at the beginning of his slumber, he'd wait until he was too tired to stay awake and then fall asleep when he could no longer fight it.

Until then he drifted in his boat, under the darkness of the lake, and hoped that one day soon he could forget about the morning in Half Moon Bay and the screams that echoed in his mind as Harrison Whitney fell to his death.

29

Alex bolted awake at two in the morning, wincing under the throbbing of his stitches, and one odd but persistent memory stabbing at his mind. Steady, continuous beeping echoed through the darkened halls, and a subtle yellow light buzzed above his head. The antiseptic smell reminded him of where he was and his breathing calmed. His hand brushed across his cheek where he could still feel the gravel that had scratched the surface of his skin. The oil and leaking garbage from the back lane still resonated, but it was another scent that he struggled to remember. It made little sense and it wasn't even clear, but the fact that he couldn't push it away made him sense its importance. He had left three messages for Peter and when he didn't return his call, he then tried to reach Kerry at Fox Lodge.

Kerry was still groggy when Mrs. Kemp shook her awake and told her a young man was calling from the hospital. Kerry looked at the message with the number Mrs. Kemp wrote down and pulled her cell phone off the night table beside the bed.

Alex answered the phone, anxiety clear in his voice, and his rapid speech made it difficult to understand what he was trying to say. Kerry knew he was on intense painkillers, which would be unavoidable considering the number of stab wounds he sustained across his back. It was always the day after a patient received stitches that the pain flares up once the numbness of the local anesthetic wears off. The tightness of the skin being pulled unnaturally closed with the suture thread feels like a fresh cut over an old bruise. The itching would be unbearable and with the injuries being on Alex's back, he probably was having difficulty finding a comfortable position to rest. And although the painkillers would help with that, it also made coherent conversation near impossible.

"His breath, his breath, his breath," Alex's tone was becoming more frustrated each time he repeated the words.

"What do you mean, 'his breath'?" Kerry tried to get Alex to be more specific.

"It smelled!" Alex was shouting now.

Kerry pulled her legs up to her chest and dropped her face onto her knees. She was still in bed and barely awake and trying to decipher Alex's ramblings.

"What did it smell like, Alex?"

Alex let out a long sigh followed by a groan, the pain from his wounds was distracting him.

"Do you want me to call you later?" Kerry asked.

"No," Alex snapped through gritted teeth. "I'm trying to tell you I remember the guy who attacked me had a smell on his breath."

"What smell? Like a burger or onions?"

"Like my grandma's lotion."

Great, Kerry thought, know we need to look for an attacker that smells of lotion.

"I'll tell Constable George when I see him today, and we'll put it in your file," Kerry promised, hoping that would relieve Alex's hysteria.

"You think I'm crazy, don't you?" Alex's voice was a little softer now and Kerry thought he sounded like he was crying.

"No, I just think it can be very traumatic when you're attacked and that memories can sometimes get jumbled, especially when you're on painkillers," Kerry explained. "Just rest and let the nurses take care of you, remember, you also lost a lot of blood."

"I'm telling you his breath smelled exactly like the lavender lotion my grandma used to use."

Kerry suddenly tuned into what Alex was trying to say and thought back to the drink that she shared with Mrs. Kemp and the scent that was always present on Harrison Whitney's breath.

She reminded Alex to rest and told him that she'd take care of getting the information to Constable George and that it may, after all, be useful. Feeling more relieved, Alex thanked her and then disconnected the call, eager himself to fall asleep.

Kerry finished dressing before Mrs. Kemp poured a cup of coffee for her, and after gulping it down, she ran down to the dock and jumped into the boat, and headed into town.

Peter arrived at the station just as Kerry ran up the stairs and she quickly explained the call she had with Alex that morning.

"As frantic and confused as I initially thought he was, I think it may help point us toward a suspect," Kerry explained.

"So, you think the scent Alex smelled on the breath of his attacker was the same smell from the gin Harrison was drinking?"

"You smelled it too," Kerry reminded Peter. "And since he seems to drink that throughout the entire day, it's no wonder that it's pretty strong anytime you're around him."

"The attack on Velma was personal, and the one person that had the most to lose from Velma was her husband," Peter turned around and walked down the stairs. "Let's go out and speak to Mr. Whitney and see if he has an alibi for the night that Alex was attacked. I did a little more digging around, and Harrison was going to inherit more money than he let on when we spoke with him earlier. In fact, he'd be a very wealthy man if his wife suddenly died."

Kerry ran down the stairs and caught up to Peter, "What motive would he have for attacking Alex though?"

"Maybe he found out that Alex and Hannah were an item and was more jealous than he let on," Peter suggested. "It wouldn't be the first time a spurned lover turned violent. Especially once his wife was out of the way. Maybe he thought that he'd have a chance for an open relationship with Hannah."

Kerry couldn't disagree. Many violent crimes were committed by individuals that the victim knew quite well or had a relationship with. Kerry could never get used to violent deaths. A grieving family was left behind, and precious lives were taken for senseless reasons. And more often than not, a murderer who regretted what he or she had done, was tormented with guilt.

Family members were often the most likely suspects in murder cases, and for good reason. Passion and upset existed between people who knew each other well, and not as often between random strangers. Harrison Whitney was in their crosshairs at the beginning of their investigation and for good reason.

However, it was Daniella and Helena that Kerry felt the greatest pain for. No matter how they approached it, they could end up losing both of their parents if their suspicions were correct.

There were several boats on the familiar trip out to Braemar Island, more than Kerry had seen on recent trips. Each boater offered a nod and a wave, which Peter explained was customary, even when you didn't know who the boaters were.

Kerry thought it was a charming practice, although she wouldn't be in Lake Pines long enough for that to be an issue.

As they neared Braemar Island, the early morning light cast a yellow shadow over the front dock and the warmth of the sun seared on the back of Kerry's neck. Kerry folded her hand across her forehead and shook the collar of her shirt. Beads of sweat trailed down her spine, and the storm warnings from the night before never transpired in rainfall.

The storm and promise of relief from the heat, circled around Lake Pines leaving thick humidity hanging in the air. The inviting sound of the water lapping against the cribs beneath the boards made her want to dive into the lake and distracted her just enough that she forgot to grab the edge of the dock.

Peter met her apologies with a smile and a shake of his head along with a promise of, "You'll learn."

They climbed onto the dock and walked toward the cottage. The quiet on the island seemed to amplify the sound of the water splashing against the rocks on the shore. Three birds fluttered into the sky when Kerry and Peter passed under the branch they were resting upon, carrying their morning song with them and leaving an eerie silence behind.

It should have been a foreboding for what awaited them ahead, but Kerry still refused to listen to her gut during times like this. Instead, she pushed them aside and tried to rely on facts to guide her.

They hadn't talked about what they would say to Harrison when he answered the door or what Peter would do if he didn't have a suitable alibi. Neither they expected would return a welcome response since it came with the accusation of his wife's murder attached to them. There was no reply to the knock on the door or the two subsequent ones that came with more force. Peter shouted inside as he opened the door, calling Harrison's name as he stepped into the cottage. They both saw him at the same time.

It was Harrison Whitney. He didn't move when they walked into the cottage, he couldn't. He lay crumpled on the floor, at the base of the stairs. They ran to where he lay, and Kerry knelt beside his head and felt for a pulse on his neck. It was faint, but it was there, and his labored breathing was low. Kerry ran her fingers along Harrison's body, checking his spine, while Peter called for a Medivac. Both Kerry and Peter were thinking the same thing, whatever happened to Harrison Whitney, they hoped it had nothing to do with Daniella.

30

The tops of the trees swirled and a flurry of leaves ripped from the branches as the emergency helicopter tried to find enough space to land on Braemar Island. Normally the sound of the rushing air and thumping of pulse of the blades brought excitement. Air churning in a myriad of directions, pulling and pushing, challenged anyone to look away. However, this time Kerry watched nervously as two paramedics jumped out and ran into the cottage. They assessed Harrison, secured his body to a board, and then radioed ahead to the hospital. A broken clavicle, three fractures on his leg, and undefined head trauma. The paramedic lowered his eyes as the injuries were explained to the emergency staff waiting at the hospital. Kerry didn't need to ask why. Harrison's injuries were severe and could be fatal.

With measured steps, the paramedics carefully carried Harrison's body out of the cottage and across the lawn and then eased him into the waiting helicopter.

Kerry watched from the window as the helicopter pilot started up the engine and the blades began to spin, picking up speed as they waited to lift off. Two police boats arrived at the same time with the forensic equipment to search for evidence inside the cottage.

When the forensic crew arrived, Kerry and Peter began directing them on what to look for as they searched the cottage.

There were signs of a struggle in the bedroom on the second floor, and Harrison's smashed phone was laying on the landing of the staircase. It didn't look like anything had been stolen, but Peter didn't want to take any shortcuts, especially since Velma was murdered just days earlier.

Kerry was holding the front door open for an officer who was returning from his boat with a camera balanced atop a large case when she saw the jacket hanging underneath a brown sweater next to the door.

"Peter, look at this," Kerry pointed to hooks next to the door. "That looks like a sailing team jacket to me."

Peter removed the sweater that was partially covering the jacket and then stretched the front of the jacket flat. The fabric had a run through the blue material on the right side of the chest area and several small rips were visible. There were also a few small dark stains on the collar of the coat which experience told Kerry, could be dried blood. They both looked at each other and wondered how Velma or Harrison's name hadn't appeared on the list of members who purchased a jacket, and how it escaped anyone's notice.

"Let's bag it and take it in, but I think we'll find it's a match."

With a gloved hand, Peter removed the jacket from the hook and held it in an outstretched arm, shaking it gently when he felt a weight inside the pocket. With his free hand, he reached into the pocket and removed a small pocket knife. It was stainless steel and had two arms that folded into the middle casing and had an engraving etched on the side. Peter unfolded one of the curved blades and held it up. The serrated edge caught Kerry's eye.

"That blade looks exactly like what could have been used to stab Alex," Kerry squinted at the writing, almost worn off with age, and tried to figure out what it said. "Can you make that out?"

Peter didn't need to take a second glance or look any closer, he had seen that logo enough throughout his life, "It's a rigging knife, and it's primarily used by sailors. The engraving you see on the side is the name of the club. It's their old logo, they haven't used it in almost ten years."

"It looks like it's been wiped clean, but I'll still check it out. If Alex was stabbed with this knife, there could still be traces in the hinges," Kerry explained. "I've yet to see a murder weapon completely wiped clean of evidence."

Peter placed both the jacket and knife in separate evidence bags. Just as Peter was sealing the bags, Daniella burst through the doors and looked at both Kerry and Peter.

"What happened? Where's my dad?" Daniella panicked. Kerry calmed Daniella down as she explained that she and her sister had spent the night at a friend's cottage. Emotions were still too heated to spend time alone with their father and they needed a night away. He had wanted them to spend the evening at Sweeny's Fishing Lodge but both she and her sister decided that the pain was still raw to spend time with him. Daniella said he had been alone all night, and they didn't know what happened.

Daniella glanced around the room, her eyes landed on the floor where a small puddle of her father's blood marked the wood. Police officers passed them carrying items in sealed plastic bags and clicks echoed as a camera captured images of the staircase from several angles. As Daniella absorbed the severity of her father's fall, her face began to flush and her pulse quickened. She clutched at her chest, pulling the fabric of her shirt tight with her fist.

Helena didn't come into the cottage, and instead, was standing on the porch, staring down at the movement on the lawn. Her eyes followed the trail of the helicopter as it lifted above the trees, and she began to cry. Her body shook, and she wrapped her thin arms around her waist and bent forward.

She was all alone.

Inside the cottage, Daniella yelled to no one in particular. She had been so angry at her mother for drinking and her father for not being there for her, and now she might be faced with a life without either of them. She wanted to shut her eyes and pretend that none of this was happening and that the police would be gone and that both of her parents, as imperfect as they both were, would both still be there with them. But one look at her father being carried away in an emergency helicopter told her that she was living her worst nightmare.

Daniella fell into Kerry's arms and began to scream.

31

Before they left Braemar Island, Kerry calmed both girls and waited with them as a friend came to pick them up.

Daniella's arms were still shaking and Helena was refused to turn her eyes away from the ground. Neither was capable of driving or thinking clearly and even though they were technically adults, at this moment Kerry knew they were simply two distraught children who were feeling terribly lost. Two police officers began dusting the cottage for prints, looking for any signs of the intruder while Kerry waited with the girls.

Once Daniella and Helena had left with their friend, Kerry searched through the cottage herself and she started in the rooms that it appeared the family used the most. Pictures, similar to the ones she saw in Byron Gray's cottage, lined the shelves of the main family room. However, unlike Byron Gray's frames, the images in the photos contained a variety of people and spanned over generations.

Next to books and games, images recorded the moments played out on Braemar Island throughout several generations. Black and white images of Wilson Pratt standing next to a timber structure frame, were the first to catch Kerry's attention. Workers in attire that resembled office suits, stood next to lengths of lumber balanced on pairs of workhorses with their sleeves rolled up with sweaty smiles under wide-brimmed hats. Five-by-six photos captured various stages of construction and were assembled in a framed collage on the wall.

Women in long skirts, some pulled up and tied around their waists, waded knee-deep off the shore to cool themselves on a warm summer day. A picture resembling the famous James Tissot's 1876 painting where elegantly dressed men and women lounged on a blanket, picnicking by a pond, was in the center of the frame. Except this wasn't an oil painting that Kerry was looking at, they were images of Velma's grandparents on the day they completed the building of the cottage she was now standing inside.

She scanned the images captured in the photos and when she reached the collection of Velma as a teenager, then as a young adult, and finally as a parent, one similarity stood out. In most photos, she had a colorful scarf wrapped around her neck, much like the ones in the photos sitting on Byron Gray's shelves. The morning that Velma was killed was foggy and a thick mist weighed down the lake, and Kerry recalled there also being a chill in the air.

It was likely that she was wearing a scarf the morning she was killed, but none was found on her body or on the beach.

Kerry searched through the cottage specifically for the same colored scarf she saw repeatedly in the photos, but she failed to find it. She moved through the cottage, running her eyes over the disturbed piles of clothing and opened drawers, and wondered what the intruder could have been looking for.

When Kerry first assessed Harrison, sweet lavender scented gin was heavy on his shallow breath and could have easily caused his fall from the second floor. However, the thickness of the oak banister defied the logic that a man of Harrison's weight could break the railing, even in a drunken stupor. It would take a hard shove or an aggressive push to send a man of Harrison Whitney's size and weight through the railing and down to the bottom of the stairs.

His phone was in an evidence bag, its screen shattered, but surprisingly the phone was still working. With no security lock code enabled, Kerry opened the phone and as the fractured screen brightened, Harrison's contact list was open and it highlighted one number, indicating who he was trying to call.

Kerry ran up the stairs and called Peter out of the bedroom where he was bagging some items he thought the intruder may have touched.

"You need to see this," Kerry turned the phone around so Peter could see the image and the number through the crumpled plastic bag and the cracked screen. "He was trying to call you. Maybe he walked in on a robbery."

"I don't think it was a robbery that Harrison Whitney walked in on," Peter said. "His wallet was on the night table and he had over two hundred dollars in it, and Velma's jewelry was on the top of the dresser where a thief could've easily just grabbed it. Whoever he walked in on was here for another reason and was looking for something specific. Most of the items that were rummaged through belonged to Velma, so it was likely that whoever was here last night was looking for something that belonged to her."

"And maybe it was what got her killed," Kerry let out a deep sigh and hoped that Harrison would survive his injuries. First, so he could be a parent to Daniella and Helena who both so desperately needed him to be, and second, so he could tell them who had attacked him since it now looked like it was probably the person who also killed his wife.

As Kerry walked down to the dock and climbed into the waiting police boat, she looked into the deep green shadow that stretched across the lawn as it shaded the water. She couldn't shake the repeated images of Velma with the brightly colored scarf, standing and smiling with friends at a barbeque. Especially the ones that were taken at Half Moon Bay, with Byron Gray standing nearby and looking on.

32

Byron Gray stood over the burning barrel throwing ripped pieces of paper onto the bright orange flames. He watched as the pages went from a stark white to brown and then eventually they folded in on themselves as they curled into a deep black. As the flames consumed the evidence against him, pieces of ash floated into the air and drifted around his head, some landing and staining his yellow shirt sleeve.

It wasn't supposed to end up like this between him and Velma. They were a perfect match for each other, better than the one Velma thought she had with Harrison. Byron had loved her for most of his life and was the reason he could never move on and settle down with anyone else. He believed that eventually Velma would see Harrison's true colors and leave him, and she almost had.

The first summer of her newly found sobriety, she confided in Byron that she was ready to stand on her own two feet and leave Harrison. Byron shielded his excitement and patiently waited for Velma to announce her divorce but year after year she failed to do so.

Yet, he continued to wait.

Two weeks ago she called him and said she needed to speak with him privately, and that it couldn't be at her cottage or the club.

Byron had put a bottle of her favorite flavored sparkling soda on ice and set two crystal glasses next to it on the table. A candle was lit, and the fire had been burning in the hearth for most of the afternoon, pine and ash scented the cottage. His mind flashed back to when they were just teenagers and the last perfect day they had together on a boat trip down the lake with a few friends, and he grew excited with the prospect of finally being open about his true feelings for her.

When she walked in and saw the presentation Byron prepared, her eyes teared up and she told him that he had misunderstood. She handed him the pages that her investigator had prepared and she told him she knew everything that he had done, and that's why she was there.

The painful realization hit him hard after so many years of pining for the only woman he cared about. Velma would never love him the way he loved her, and that he had wasted his life waiting for things to change. That was only two weeks ago, but after everything that happened, Byron thought it felt like a lifetime. He couldn't sleep and nightmares and painful memories constantly awoke him as they crept into his mind.

Byron shook the memory of the awkwardness of that afternoon from his mind and the subsequent argument and tears that followed. Instead, he gathered the documents she had given him and tore them into small pieces, and tossed them on the fire. Once every piece of evidence was burned, he laid Velma's top on the fire as well. He had saved it from when they had gone on that boat trip when they were eighteen. She had left it behind on his boat and assumed it was lost, but Byron had kept it as a memento of his affection and as a reminder of that one perfect day they shared.

Considering everything that had happened over the last few days, Byron couldn't risk being caught with a piece of her clothing and he laid it on the fire. Tears streamed down his face as he watched the flames grab the seam of the light green cotton shirt and he hoped as it burned that he could find a way to move on, and away, from Velma's death.

33

Circumstance or fate. One of them brought Harrison Whitney to the hospital where Kerry was waiting with Peter for a report on his condition.

It was a couple of hours before Doctor Weisz emerged to speak with them.

"Mr. Whitney is unconscious right now, and it may be the best place for him to be considering the fall he took. Besides the swelling on his brain, his leg is fractured in three areas and his left shoulder was dislocated," Doctor Weisz shifted his feet and stretched his back.

"When, or if, he comes to, he's going to be in a lot of pain."

Doctor Weisz agreed to call Peter the moment Harrison woke up. Kerry promised to relay the information to his daughters, who she said were resting at a friends' cottage.

"Good," Doctor Weisz said. "It's probably better that they're not waiting in the hospital. It can be especially stressful for family members."

While Harrison was being cared for by Doctor Weisz, Kerry went to the lab and examined the regatta jacket that they found at his cottage. Small tears and pulls of the material could easily have been caused by Velma's ring, lodging the small blue fiber in the clasp of her diamond.

Samples of the dark stains on the collar of the jacket came back as an exact match to Velma Whitney's blood. This was the missing regatta jacket that they had been looking for and was what the murderer was wearing the morning that Velma Whitney was killed.

Kerry also had no difficulty finding traces of blood in the small recesses of the folding rigging knife. Under a magnifying lens and with the use of small medical swabs, she removed samples of dried blood from inside the casing.

Results were conclusive. They were an exact match for Alex's blood type.

Kerry closed her eyes and rubbed her lids. The only thing left to do was to wait for either Harrison Whitney to wake up and tell them who attacked him, or for

Peter's officers to find evidence of who was at the cottage the night he was attacked.

The jacket and the knife both suggested that Harrison was responsible for both crimes, but what didn't make sense was who attacked him.

It was only moments before she and Peter arrived at Braemar Island that they believed that Harrison could be a suspect in both his wife's murder as well as the attack on Alex. Finding the jacket and knife just made his guilt more plausible, however, discovering Harrison Whitney at the bottom of his stairs put their assumptions in doubt.

Now, there was another suspect they needed to identify, which obscured their investigation.

The scent of the gin that Harrison drank on a regular, maybe even daily basis, was identical to the scent that Alex remembered smelling the night he was attacked in the alley behind his apartment. Peter had stopped by Alex's room in the hospital and asked him to smell the sample that was collected at the Whitney cottage, and he confirmed that was in fact the scent he remembered smelling.

Unfortunately for Harrison, he was also looking more like the only person who would have benefited from his wife's death. Not only was he having an affair, but his claim that he would only receive a small annuity had also proved to be false.

Specifically, Harrison would receive one million dollars upon Velma's death, and then two-hundred-thousand annually for the remainder of his life.

Money was often the crux to many crimes, and murder wasn't immune to the power of greed. Freedom from his marriage and the funds to live well would have both been motivating factors in seeing his wife killed.

Harrison had lied about benefiting financially from his wife's death, that much was obvious. But why?

Most spouses received funds from a life insurance policy, which wouldn't have caused any suspicions. But by being deceitful about it, Harrison only succeeded in angling guilt in his direction.

Kerry recalled the wound on Velma's head, and the marks on the back of her neck that exposed a struggle in the last moments of her life. It was an impassioned murder, and one filled with rage, and she couldn't help but wonder what kind of anger caused Velma's death?

The buzzing of her phone disrupted the silence in the lab. For once, Kerry welcomed the distraction and answered the phone when she saw it was Jean calling from Montreal.

She greeted her old boss in her poor, broken French that he often chided her for and then followed with a yawn.

"I thought you were in Lake Pines to rest?" Jean joked. "Hopefully your exhaustion is because you are at least having fun?"

Kerry first apologized for not calling Jean sooner and then explained the events that transpired over her last few days in Lake Pines.

"Ah, then that explains it," Jean said.

"Explains what?"

"My secretary received a call from a Doctor Crampton from Lake Pines. He was calling to get a reference on your work history and to find out about the cases you worked on," Jean explained. "I was surprised because I thought you were planning on moving to Vancouver. I didn't know you were looking to stay in Lake Pines?"

"He what?"

Jean explained that he assumed Doctor Crampton was calling for a reference and seemed confused about Kerry's upset.

"Jean, I'll have to call you back," Kerry tried to calm her breathing as she spoke.

"What about Vancouver?" Jean asked. "Doctor Burton will need to know soon Kerry. I'll see if I can get him to hold off for a while, considering you're in the middle of a case right now."

Kerry promised to make her decision soon and to call Jean when she did.

As soon as she ended the call, she burst out of the lab and into Doctor Crompton's office without knocking on the door or waiting to be invited inside.

"Why were you calling Montreal about my work record?" Kerry screamed. She could feel her face warm and knew her neck would soon be streaked with the telltale red lines she was known for.

"Kerry, let me explain," Doctor Crompton walked around his desk and closed the door to his office.

"Explain what? How you invaded my privacy."

"It's not like that," he sat down in the chair in front of his desk and asked Kerry to take the other.

"I'll admit I was upset when I first made the call to Montreal. Mad, actually. I thought you stepped over the line when you disagreed with what I thought Velma Whitney's cause of death was," Doctor Crampton leaned back in the chair, looking exhausted and tired. "I learned a lot about your time in Montreal when you worked for Jean Lamont. I learned how you graduated top of your class, that you were instrumental in finding evidence in several cases that led to convictions, and I also learned why you left your job."

It was Kerry's turn to fall back into the chair, and she paused for a long while before she spoke. "Then you know why I needed to take some time off. I still blame myself for what happened."

"It may surprise you to learn that I had the same thing happen to me when I was just starting out in Lake Pines," Doctor Crampton admitted. "I, too, had a hard time forgiving myself."

"What changed?" Kerry asked, holding back the tears that always came when she remembered the case where she failed the young murder victim.

"I realized that there were more cases that needed my help."

Kerry looked down at her lap and closed her eyes and felt Doctor Crampton's hand fall on her arm.

"It's not your fault, Kerry. You're a good doctor and you were right to call me out down at the dock."

Kerry raised her face and saw Doctor Crampton smiling. He apologized for his quick temper and the anger and distrust he unfairly judged her with. He not only thanked her for her help with Velma Whitney's murder but was appreciative for the reminder that even though he had a lifetime of great cases behind him, that he couldn't let down his guard for one moment.

"Every victim deserves justice," Doctor Crampton declared with a gentle smile.

Silence settled between them for a few moments while both Kerry and Doctor Crampton came to terms with their newly acquired respect for each other. They no longer had the antagonistic tension that existed from the first moment they met on the dock the day Velma Whitney's body was found. Almost watching it disappear before their eyes.

It was Doctor Crampton who broke the silence, "What did you find on the jacket?"

Happy to return their focus to Velma Whitney's case, Kerry explained the evidence she found of both the rip in the jacket as well as Velma's blood on the collar. She also informed him that the knife was also a match for the attack on Alex which put Harrison in a whole new light, regardless of the injuries that sent him to the hospital.

"I just don't know how the Whitney's having an extra jacket missed the list we received."

Doctor Crampton smiled, "That's easy. If it's anything like the time I coached my son's softball team, the company always sends out a couple of sample jackets before a team places an order. Maybe it was one of those jackets. You should call the manufacturer and see if there were any samples sent out before any orders were placed?"

Kerry thanked Doctor Crampton and rushed out of his office to tell Peter. Doctor Crampton proved something today in his office, that there was no replacement for his experience or a lifetime of knowledge.

As Kerry ran down the hall, she yelled back to Doctor Crampton, "You may have just solved this case!"

34

Finding Harrison Whitney's crumpled body at the bottom of his staircase changed her mind about his guilt, however, that also put them back to square one and Kerry hoped that what Doctor Crampton said about the jackets would be enough to reveal another viable suspect. She called Peter as she was running across the street to the police station and she was eager to find out if there were any sample jackets, and if so, who had them. Peter told Kerry to meet him at the docks and that they'd go out to the club to see if Paul could get them the names of anyone who may have received a sample jacket.

They arrived at the Channel Island Summer Club just as Paul was leaving his office after meeting with Sally Gale and Heath Middleton. Paul smiled as Peter and Kerry rushed through the front doors and called his name.

"Paul, is there any chance you have the master list from the supplier for every sailing jacket that was ordered?" Peter asked. "Including any samples?"

"Yeah, they're in my desk," Paul opened the door to his office and walked back inside. "Let me get them."

"No you won't," Heath Middleton interrupted. "This has gone on long enough. You can't show up every time you want to see private information. We answered all of your questions, and you even got access to our security camera I understand, which by the way shouldn't have happened, and now you want to see personal information on some of our members!"

"We just want to know who had the jackets, including any of the samples that may have been sent," Peter explained.

"Why? So you can pin a murder on them?" Heath crossed his arms, flourishing in his legal element. Heath glared at Peter and held only slightly more than a sneer when he spoke. "Get a warrant and we'd be happy to release any of the files, until then, Mr. Jensen will be keeping them safe in his office."

Peter had come face to face before with lawyers when they insisted on sanctioned warrants and he knew that there was no way around it. He held back the protest he wanted to make, knowing they could only hold it against him if they needed them in court. They drove into town and to the police station where they would call the judge on duty and get a warrant. And hopefully, they could get it tonight and finally find out who may have killed Velma Whitney.

35

Guy Stanton was waiting in the front lobby when they arrived back at the station. The receptionist offered to take his name and number, but he insisted on waiting.

The receptionist waved Kerry over as soon as she walked through the door, "That man has been waiting here for an hour, and he didn't want to leave a message."

"Who is it?" Kerry didn't recognize the man.

"He says his name is Guy Stanton, and that you wanted to see him," the receptionist shrugged her shoulders and said that was all the information she was able to extract and they were now left with a man sitting in the waiting area for the last hour.

Kerry walked over to him and introduced herself and asked why he had been looking for her, thinking there must be some mistake.

"Josie said you wanted me to call you when I came back into town," Guy explained and when a look of confusion crossed Kerry's face he added with a whisper, "about Velma."

"Oh," Kerry said, realizing that this was the man whom Velma spoke to at her meetings. "Come with me."

Kerry walked over to where Peter was standing and whispered, "Do you have a moment?"

Peter nodded, "Let's go back to my office."

Kerry guided Guy down the hall and into Peter's office and then closed the door. Guy was a tall thin man and wore a three-day-old beard, one that made Kerry think he had a trimmer permanently set to a number two setting. His jeans were well worn on the thighs, and he wore a flannel shirt unbuttoned over a stark white t-shirt, and the retro logo on his turned-around cap reminded her of one her father wore.

"How can I help you?" Peter put his jacket over the back of his chair and sat down.

"I'm a little confused," Guy said. "Josie said you wanted to talk to me about Velma."

Kerry nodded.

"She also said that she died?" Guy asked. "Is that true?"

"I'm afraid so," Kerry offered her condolences and sensed that Velma and Guy were friends, but nothing more.

"Man, that's so hard to believe," Guy removed his hat and ran his long fingers through his thick hair. "She was doing so well and getting her life back on track. She was a real class act."

"When was the last time you spoke with Velma?" Peter asked.

Guy widened his eyes as he flipped a mental calendar in his mind, "Oh, about two weeks ago. Why?"

"Velma didn't just die, she was murdered," Peter explained.

"We understand you were one of the few people Velma spoke with at the meetings," Kerry asked. "We wondered if you noticed anything out of the ordinary or if she mentioned being worried the last time you spoke."

Guy was looking down at his hands, and fidgeting with the visor on his cap, "Velma knew from some things I talked about during our meetings that I was an investigator for an insurance company, and she approached me about something she wanted me to look into."

"Was it her husband's debts?" Kerry asked.

"No, she found out about those when one of her friends who Harrison owed money to approached her. She did her own digging and found the court records," Guy explained. "She apparently paid everyone off so they'd drop their claims against her husband."

"Was she upset about that?"

"At first, but then eventually she came to terms with it," Guy let out a chuckle. "She said that after everything she put him through when she was drinking that it was the least she could do to help him out. She never wanted him to know about her settling all the debts because she just wanted to focus on their marriage. She really loved him. She even told me she wanted to sell their cottage and go somewhere that they could start over and hopefully repair their marriage."

"Did she tell you he was having an affair?"

Guy nodded, "She knew about all of them, but she wanted to forgive him and move on."

"Then why did Velma hire you?" Peter asked. "If it wasn't about her husband's debts or his affair?"

"She had me look into the Channel Island Summer Club's Executive Members," Guy shook his head. "Specifically their finances. She had an inkling that someone was scraping money off the books and she wanted to know who it was. She was planning on leaving her position as the treasurer at the end of this summer and wanted to make sure that she left the club, and the books, in good shape."

"Were you able to find anything out for her?" Kerry had already guessed the name that Guy was about to say, just as she assumed Peter had as well.

"At first glance, everything seemed on the up and up. The payroll records were balanced with the timesheets and all the receipts for the supplies were in order, but when I dug deeper, I realized the person responsible had added nine names to the payroll for people who didn't actually work there. He added member's kid's names to the payroll list, and then signed off on paying them cash, which most kids prefer in the summer so it didn't look odd at first," Guy explained. "When I gave her the report I think she was more upset at the name I uncovered as opposed to the theft itself."

"Who did you find out was stealing money?"

"The Activities Coordinator, Byron Gray."

36

It was Helena who was sitting next to her father's bed when he began to stir. Daniella walked into the room as her sister was crying and holding her father's hand as he smiled and stroked her soft hair with his other one. He looked up and saw Daniella and reached out for her to join them and she rushed to his side.

The nurse walked in when she heard the commotion and called the doctor who ran in behind her. After a brief examination, Doctor Weisz left Harrison with his two daughters while he called Peter.

Peter was away from the station, on his way to speak with Byron Gray, and Officer Jones offered to come to the hospital to speak with Harrison Whitney. Harrison's leg was elevated in a sling, and a pile of pillows crowded around his shoulders and neck as he spoke with his daughters.

The officer introduced himself and after apologizing for Peter's absence, he asked him about the accident that sent him through his banister and into the hospital.

"I understand that it was Constable George who found me?" Harrison's voice was scratchy and weak.

Officer Jones nodded, "Yes, it's a good thing he and Doctor Dearborne arrived when they did."

Officer Jones briefly explained what Constable George thought happened as well as the state of the cottage when they searched for evidence to who may have attacked him. He also explained the two pieces of evidence they found that connected directly to both his wife's murder and the attack on Alex Berg.

"We weren't aware that you also had a sailing jacket?" It was a comment, posed as a question.

The three Whitney faces looked back at the officer with a perplexed glare.

"No one in our family has one of the club sailing jackets, as a matter of fact, no one in our family has ever sailed," Harrison said. "Not even Velma."

Officer Jones hadn't been involved as deeply in the investigation, but he was briefed on the file and understood the importance of Harrison's comment. He realized that the jacket and knife were planted there as a setup and that the intruder had probably placed them there.

"Did you happen to get a glimpse of the man who attacked you?" the officer asked.

Harrison wasn't a fan or a friend of the man, however, he also never would have thought he'd be the one to harm Velma.

Harrison nodded. Ever since he first met the man, he always felt a sting of disapproval or even jealousy at his being in Velma's life. Harrison had always brushed off the extra attention he gave Velma as just another one of her summer lake admirers and never worried about committing his name to memory or adding it to his list of close friends. But when he told Officer Jones the name of the man who attacked him after he caught him rummaging through Velma's drawers, he knew his name would be seared into his memory as the person who took his one true love.

37

The police arrived at Byron's cottage just as the crash echoed through the cottage.

Peter ran up the steps with Kerry close behind. The muffled shouts followed the sound of crashing glass and tables being knocked over. They burst through the doors just as Byron Gray was being thrown to the ground by a man who had both of his hands wrapped around his throat. Bryon's legs kicked furiously against the weight of his attacker and Peter was quickly behind them, pulling the attacker off Byron.

They both crashed to the floor and within a few seconds Peter had the attacker face down with his knee in his back and Kerry was on the ground next to Byron making sure he was alright.

Blood trickled down the edge of Byron's mouth and he coughed vigorously as he tried to catch his breath. Kerry helped him to his feet and then guided him to a chair and made him sit.

It wasn't the scene that Kerry had expected to walk in on, and when Peter flipped Byron's attacker over, the face was one she hadn't expected to see.

Paul squeezed his lips tight and dropped his head. He tried to remember the words his father told him, *protect your family*.

38

Paul Jensen was panting as he leaned forward, shaking his head and holding back sobs. His hands were cuffed behind his back and Peter was trying to make sense of what he had just walked in on.

"Do you want to tell me what's going on?" Peter's commanding voice echoed through the small cottage.

Paul shook his head and bit down on his bottom lip.

"Is this about the money Byron has been stealing from the club?" Peter asked.

Paul lifted his head and looked at Peter, shocked at hearing Byron was stealing money from the club, but then the anger passed and he shook his head.

"Paul, you have to give me something," Peter begged. "Why did I just have to pull you off of Byron?"

"I'll tell you why," Bryon jumped up from the chair, and with Paul safely restrained by handcuffs, he walked toward him and Peter. "It's because I found out what he'd done!"

Peter and Kerry looked at Byron, both with confused looks on their faces.

"I found her scarf in his drawer and it was covered in blood," Byron was shouting, and spittle was collecting on the corners of his mouth, and the more he spoke, the angrier he became. "I was at the club early one morning and was looking in his drawer for the key to the sailing shed when I saw the corner sticking out from the back of the drawer. It was the scarf I bought for her when I was in Italy, so I know it was hers."

Bryon lunged at Paul, and Peter had to jump between them to stop Bryon from hitting him again. Peter forced Byron to sit down and to explain everything, "From the beginning."

Byron took a deep breath and explained while wiping away his tears that Velma always found the morning chill difficult to take and would often wear a scarf or a sweater pulled up around her neck. The morning she died there was a chilly fog and a thick mist in the air, he remembered because it was difficult to see driving his boat when he arrived at the club early to pick up his race gear.

As Byron spoke, Kerry thought back to the images of Velma with a brightly colored scarf wrapped around her neck, and her own instinct that maybe she had been wearing it on the morning she was killed.

Byron reluctantly admitted he always loved Velma, and although she never returned more than a friendship, he continued to care for her deeply. It was on one of his trips to Europe that he spotted the hand-painted scarf and thought of Velma and knew it would look perfect wrapped around her neck. He knew that Harrison never bought Velma little gifts, and it was something that hurt her since she mentioned it often.

The scarf was one of her favorites and he recognized the familiar colors as he pulled it out from the back of Paul's drawer. At first, Byron thought Velma had lost it and that Paul was holding on to it for her, but when he saw it stained with blood, he knew it had something to do with Velma's murder.

"I called Paul and confronted him about the scarf and he couldn't hide the guilt in his voice when I mentioned Velma's name," Byron took a deep breath and choked back his tears. "I told him I was going to tell Harrison and together we were going to go to the police, I just thought he owed it to her family to come clean, and I'd hoped he'd do it himself."

"So, what happened? Why didn't you come straight to me?" Peter asked.

"I was pulling up to Harrison's dock when someone was being carried off in the emergency helicopter, and I knew that Paul had probably done something to Harrison," Byron stabbed a glare at Paul as he spoke. "I rushed back here to get the scarf I hid in my cottage and I was going to take it directly to you and that's when Paul burst in and attacked me."

Byron stood and walked to a large cabinet and pulled out three books from the shelf, behind in a large plastic zip sealed bag, was the colorful scarf that Velma Whitney had been wearing the morning she was killed. And it was stained dark with blood.

39

They arrived at the police station, not with Byron in handcuffs, but Paul Jensen. Officer Jones was just about to call Peter when they walked into the station and immediately placed Paul into a holding cell while the details of his arrest were worked out.

"I was just trying to call you," Officer Jones was vaguely aware of Byron Gray who followed Kerry and Peter into the station. "Harrison Whitney woke up and identified Paul Jensen as the man who pushed him over the banister."

"I know," Peter tilted his head toward an upset and disheveled-looking Byron Gray. "We walked in while Mr. Jensen was attacking Mr. Gray and learned everything that happened. We even found Velma Whitney's bloodied scarf."

Kerry held the sealed bag with Velma's bloodied scarf inside and guided Byron to a chair and found him a bag of ice. The bruise had already formed where a lump had risen. Red marks and small bruises streaked the edge of Byron's neck where Paul's fingers squeezed his throat.

Paul still refused to speak, and it was Byron who gave Peter the name and phone number of his wife and daughter. Kerry looked to Peter with the same surprised shocked glare he returned to her.

"Hannah is Paul's daughter?" Kerry said. "How did that not come up?"

Byron shrugged his shoulders.

Peter spent an hour in an interrogation room with Paul, while Officer Jones recorded their conversation, but he refused to speak or answer any questions about Velma. When his wife, Alice, arrived with Hannah, they were accompanied by a lawyer who insisted on speaking with Paul in private before he answered any more questions. And Kerry noticed that his lawyer wasn't Heath Middleton.

Paul Jensen was formally charged with the attempted murder of Byron Gray and Harrison Whitney along with the murder of Velma Whitney. He knew that he would need more evidence to charge him with the attack on Alex Berg, which he was certain Paul was responsible for as well.

Filing paperwork was the second least favorite thing in Peter's job, the first, of course, was finding a dead body.

Kerry had dropped off the bloodied scarf at the lab and Doctor Crampton insisted that he run the tests. He admitted he was feeling tired and that he may have let that interfere with his initial assessment of Velma Whitney's cause of death.

"I owe it to her, Kerry," Doctor Crampton said as he gently took the bag, and with a smile, he went into the back room in his lab and began to test the scarf and the dried blood which everyone was certain would be a match to Velma Whitney.

Kerry walked the short distance to the police station to wait with Peter for the results when Mary Jonnasen came into the station looking for them both.

"Daniella gave me your names," she was breathing heavily and she apologized for being out of breath. "I ran all the way from the dock."

Kerry pulled out a chair and Peter grabbed a bottle of water from the fridge and handed it to her.

"I'm not exactly sure what it is I can do for you?" Peter asked, not recognizing her name or face.

"You have it wrong," Mary explained. "I think I can help you."

Peter listened as Mary briefly explained her long-standing friendship with Velma and the close bond they shared.

"We told each other everything. She knew that I was pregnant before my husband did, and I knew about hers before Harrison. We have always been close, and in addition to sharing the wonderful moments in our life, we shared the bad ones too," Mary took a deep breath before she continued. "It was about a month ago that I got a call from Velma. She was trying to make things right with some people she thought she hurt. In the process, she stumbled upon some terrible things that other people were doing. I told her to leave it alone and to just focus on her own healing, but she wouldn't listen. She didn't want to leave it alone."

"Was this about the money that was being stolen from the club's finances?" Kerry asked.

Mary nodded, "Among other things. Velma had a feeling that the finances didn't match up with what they recorded on the club's books so she had a private investigator look into it. Someone she met at one of her meetings."

"Guy Stanton," Kerry said.

"Yeah, that's him," Mary confirmed. "Anyway, it was pretty easy to figure out that Byron was skimming money from the club's books, but when Velma confronted him about it, he promised to repay it all by the end of the summer. His business had taken a downturn and he was too embarrassed to let anyone know. Velma promised to help him with an interest-free loan but she wanted him to make things right at the club first."

"How did Paul Jensen become involved?"

"When Velma was going over the books, she noticed a sizeable amount of fertilizer being purchased under the club account. Like all orders, they'd be picked up in town and then put into the storage area next to the sailing shed."

"Why would that have been a problem?" Kerry asked. "It seems like an innocuous purchase."

"Except the club doesn't have more than a couple hundred square feet of lawn, and there was enough fertilizer to cover several football fields. Plus, the club stopped using chemical-based products because of their commitment to water sustainability, so Velma thought it was quite suspicious and she was going to check it out."

"Do you have any idea what, if anything came of that?"

Mary shook her head, "No, but when Daniella told me that Velma was killed on Wolf Island I became suspicious myself."

"Why's that?" Kerry asked. "Both of her daughters said it was a popular place she went hiking or even just to think?"

Mary laughed, "Velma never hiked a day in her life. There was only one reason she would have been on that island, and that was to retrieve something she hid at the top of the rock peak."

Kerry looked to Peter and then back at Mary, and she explained.

"When we were teens, we used to climb to the top of that rocky peak on the island and we found a small cavern, and realized it was the perfect spot to hide stuff."

"Like what kind of things?"

"For teens that meant cigarettes or a few bottles of beer we would snag from our parents' fridges, but if Velma was up there, she may have used that same cavern to hide whatever it was that she was killed for."

40

Mary wiped away the tears as Peter drifted the boat into Half Moon Bay. The memories of her friend came flooding back along with the thought of the fear she must have felt in the final moments of her life in a place she loved above all others.

It wasn't fair. Velma had come so far along a tough road, only to have it come to a brutal end. This was the ultimate gift that Mary could give her friend, and she'd make sure that whoever killed her would pay the price.

Peter pulled the boat up onto the beach and they all jumped from the boat onto the sandy island shore. Cheerful squawks from cormorants echoed in the curved bay and reminded Mary why she and Velma loved to spend time on the island.

Removed from the greed of investors and protected by the natural preservation laws, the rocky island at Half Moon Bay was a place of respite. It was a nod to the past when cottagers came to the lake to relax and enjoy nature, and not try to control it with artificial structures and forms blown into the sides of Canadian Shield, ripping into the landscape, and reaching out into the pristine lake with disfigured docks and boathouses. Like gnarled claws, spoiling the peace of the land and visually distorting its features.

Mary walked directly to the path that she and Velma used to climb to the top of the rocky peak, not realizing she was passing over the spot her friend had died.

Kerry and Peter followed her up, finding small ledges and nooks in the rock to place their feet and hands as they climbed. The light breeze on the beach built up to a strong wind the closer they came to their destination.

The sun ricocheted off the water and a flock of birds swooped over the bay before they came to rest on the top of some trees, fresh with new leaves and swaying gently in the wind. They came to rest at a plateau near the top, and Mary moved a collection of larger stones revealing the small cavern she and Velma used in their youth as a hiding spot.

Inside was a plastic box, protected from the elements and large enough to hold several files. Mary reached in and pulled it out. She looked at it momentarily and then handed it to Peter.

"If Velma was on this island that morning, it was to get this," Mary explained. "Whoever killed her, did so before she could retrieve it and hopefully it can shed some light on why she was murdered."

Peter rested the box on his lap and opened the lid. Inside were files of receipts, photographs, and documents that Velma had compiled against Paul.

Suddenly Peter realized what had driven him to attack her the morning she died, and what had been at stake.

And what had ultimately compelled Paul to murder his friend.

41

The tests on the scarf revealed that it not only had Velma's blood on it but Paul's as well. Velma had been able to get a couple of good punches in before he killed her. The cut to his lip was enough to draw blood and during their struggle, it dripped down onto her scarf, where the blood from her head wound also landed.

A complete search of his office and cottage found the receipt for the two jackets that Paul received as a sample from the manufacturer as well as a small tin boat whose seam matched up with the marks left on the beach. The boat was stored in Paul's boathouse on a lift since the morning he killed Velma and there were traces of her blood on the hull where he grabbed the side.

When confronted with the evidence, Paul stared blankly at the floor and let out a low, almost inaudible cry.

Velma only stumbled upon Paul's plan by accident when she was trying to balance the club's books. Large purchases of fertilizer stood out on the list of burgers, drinks, lifejackets, and rope. When she looked inside the shed and couldn't find any fertilizer supplies, she asked Alex where he had stored them, since his name was recorded as having picked them up in town.

After searching through the logbook, Alex told Velma that it wasn't him but

Paul who had gone into town to pick up supplies since those were his regular days off. Velma obtained Steven Davidson's name after searching Paul's office and found the receipt for fertilizer in his drawer. After she threatened to go to the police, Steven confessed to helping Paul with his plan.

Steven Davidson was the supplier that Paul had contacted, and it wasn't fertilizer that he had purchased. It was secretly manufactured DDT, which was banned from use since 1972. Paul funneled the purchase through the club, hoping it wouldn't be traced back to him. He began to spread the chemical on Wolf Island as well as on his neighbors' property a few years ago. Soon plants began dying and wildlife disappeared. The previously happy cottage owners who were resistant to selling were now eagerly looking to alleviate themselves of what they thought was a toxic property. Paul privately purchased the properties under his corporation's name and all that was standing in his way were the eagles and cormorants that were protected by government legislation because of their nests on Wolf Island.

Once they were killed off, there would be nothing standing in his path in having the island rezoned and available for sale, at which time he would purchase the property and begin development. Three council members had already accepted bribes and agreed to vote in Paul's favor for rezoning.

Paul stood to make millions from the property, and he used his position as the club President to shield his purchases and secret meetings with council members.

However, when Velma found out about his plans, she was determined to stop him.

Eventually, Paul did speak and he confessed to Velma's murder. The combined guilt of needing to offer Daniella and Helena some peace together with the recurring vision of Velma's lifeless body, which visited him every night, prompted Paul to explain his reasons.

It wasn't about the club finances or Velma's threats at revealing the affairs that Hannah was having with several men at the club. It was about profit, and the land Paul was looking to develop.

Velma knew about Harrison's extramarital affairs and had thought he had stopped cheating. When she found out he was having an affair with Hannah, Velma confronted her one night at the club and they argued. Hannah taunted Velma and told her that Harrison was going to leave her, and when Velma just laughed, Hannah did the unthinkable. She lied and told Velma she was pregnant with Harrison's baby. Paul found out and tried to smooth over the friction and confessed to Velma that Hannah was lying and that she was just trying to hurt her, and he begged her to leave the matter alone.

That was when Velma told Paul what she had found out about his actions with the Lake Pines council and she vowed that she wasn't going to let him get away with it.

She threatened to reveal everything after the regatta and Paul had tried to talk to her that morning hoping to change her mind.

He followed her to Wolf Island and had planned to just speak with her, the attack and her murder were both an accident. He tried to conceal the crime by pushing her body out into the lake and hoped it would drift through the channel and down the lake. He never imagined it would float into Lake Pines Bay and surface during the opening ceremonies of the club's regatta.

Charges against Paul were expanded, and the documents that proved what Paul was doing, along with blackmailing the council members to vote in his favor for the rezoning of Wolf Island, were handed over to the local prosecutors.

Paul folded his handcuffed palms together and dropped his head in defeat. It was over and he could no longer deny what happened, he just hoped his family could forgive him one day.

42

Everyone knew that Velma wouldn't have wanted to be buried in Toronto, but instead, would prefer a small service of remembrance that would take place at the lake. Byron Gray oversaw the memorial making sure that Daniella and Helena knew how much Velma loved them and that no matter what they decided to do, that everyone would be there for them as they moved forward.

A procession of antique wooden boats with their rear flags at half-mast, weaved their way around islands, through channels and circled the harbor of Lake Pines before they returned to Channel Island Summer Club for a private service. It was a solemn act of remembrance matched by the stillness of the lake and the silence in the air.

Wisps of clouds brushed across the light blue sky refusing to shield the sun, and rays bounced off the ripples of the lake adding to the serenity of the moment.

Kerry and Peter watched from a distance, choosing to offer their respects in silence as Velma's family and friends celebrated her life together.

Daniella, Helena, Harrison, and Mary went alone to Wolf Island where they spread Velma's ashes. Exactly as her Will had stipulated.

They established a fund that saw the permanent protection and nature preservation for the island which would be renamed in her mother's honor. Official charts would now read Whitney Island and it would come to represent everything that Velma loved about the lake.

Kerry also had to make the final preparations for her departure and Peter had tried for several days to change her mind. He found her help invaluable with the case and Doctor Crampton hadn't complained about her work in his lab which was his tacit compliance with her presence. This, Peter confirmed, was going to be as close as Kerry would get to a welcoming acceptance, but she held the conversation she had with him in secret, preferring to keep that moment to themselves.

She had to admit that no matter how hard she tried she could never quite remove the urge to get involved with the investigation. Once Velma Whitney floated up from under the dock, Kerry was dragged back into the exact profession and career, she thought she was running away from.

Now she saw that what she was running from wasn't the job or even the cases, but the feeling of failure that followed her around like a long dark shadow.

The realization became clear. That if Kerry was going to step into a new life, it had to be in a position where she had more control and could make a difference, and unfortunately, she wasn't sure that she'd be able to find that in Lake Pines. Doctor Burton was eager for an answer, and to offer Kerry the position, and agreed to extend the date until the end of August to give her time to think, and in the meantime, he would continue interviewing other candidates.

Simon returned to Fox Lodge the same day that Paul Jensen was arrested for the murder of Velma Whitney. News of the murder and the man responsible left Simon speechless, and he wasted no time in pouring out the rest of the lavender gin that Paul had made and given him a year earlier.

Stories turned away from the murder and to the canoe trip, and Simon shared enthusiastic reports of their time in the wilderness, each story and recounting of their time on the lake encouraged Kerry to extend her departure for an additional month. She wanted to experience the outdoors and the warmth of Lake Pines before she left, and didn't want her final memory of the area to be of Paul Jensen being led away in handcuffs and the Whitney family in shambles.

Both Simon and Mrs. Kemp were elated with her decision and Kerry couldn't help but feel touched. Mrs. Kemp was thrust into celebration mode and began to plan an afternoon barbeque at the lodge and Simon promised to spend the remaining time Kerry had in Lake Pines treating her to a personalized guided tour.

In addition to an overnight canoe trip, water skiing lessons, and regular shore lunches on the lake, Kerry grew excited at the idea of spending time alone with

Simon and she began to sense that he did as well.

The month quickly passed, and Kerry became more attached to Lake Pines and began to dread the idea of leaving the area and the people. There was, however, the matter of a job and Kerry couldn't put that off for too long, and the day finally arrived that she needed to begin to plan to move forward.

The Wi-Fi connection, as well as the coffee, was strong at Joe Black's coffee shop in the center of town and Kerry carried both her laptop and nervousness as she walked up the steep hill from the Main Street dock where she would meet Simon before she began her online search.

Simon would be waiting at the coffee shop at the top of the hill, anxiously wondering if she would show for their date. Kerry smiled. She could even picture him tapping the ends of his fingers on the surface of the table which she learned he had a habit of doing when he was nervous, just as she did. And an excitement built deep inside as she neared the front door of the coffee shop. And suddenly a wave of realization swept over her. She was truly happy.

Before she walked inside, she needed to do one more thing. She called Doctor Burton and formally declined the job offer in Vancouver. As much as she appreciated the consideration, she just wasn't ready to leave Lake Pines.

A feeling of comfort and of warmth washed over her when she ended the call, then again as she stepped inside and saw the look on Simon's face as he waved to her from across the café. She felt happy and safe, and at least for a little while, Lake Pines could possibly be home.

THE END

Author's Note

Lake Pines is a fictional town but one inspired by the beauty and the rawness of Northwestern Ontario. It is a region of Canada where I spent many years with our young family during the summer months, introduced to me by my husband, and where our boys fostered a passionate attachment to Lake of the Woods and all that it entails. During that time many experiences have been rooted in my memory and serve as the catalyst in creating the town of Lake Pines.

The simple act of breaking the surface of the waters of Lake of the Woods is a cathartic performance. I began to crave my hours swimming in the lake, feeling instantly that I was transported into a Group of Seven painting. I can close my eyes and still feel the water ripple over my arms with each stroke.

The feel of the reeds against my toes as I swam over the weed bay, ignoring the visual of a Muskie that may have possibly (and most likely) been swimming below. Then there were the stories of generations of families that vacation at the lake and the interconnected relationship between them and the permanent residents of the town that formed an essential part of our country, and they were stored as muses for the characters that were created in Lake Pines.

Bringing the atmosphere into the Lake Pines Series is a way to share a part of Canada that I love so dearly.

Murder At First Light is the (new) first book in the Lake Pines Mystery Series, having replaced the original *Murder On The Water* which didn't properly introduce Dr. Kerry Dearborne. It is a new story with a fresh plot but just introduces the characters in keeping with the Lake Pines Mystery Series.

The series was created from the unique melding of seasonal and permanent residents in the small Northwestern Ontario town and, both the series and the characters have been well-received around the world.

Thank you for reading, and I sincerely hope you enjoyed *Murder At First Light*, the (new) first book in the Lake Pines Mystery Series, and welcome you to explore the other books in the series.

So, if you enjoyed the book, please tell your friends and family, and if it isn't too much trouble, I would appreciate a brief review. And if you're on social media. . . I would love to have you follow along.

My best to you and yours.
L.L. Abbott

Books by L.L. Abbott

Mystery & Suspense

Thrillers

Teen & Young Adult

General Fiction